THE LANGUAGE OF BIRDS

ABOUT THE AUTHOR

NORBERT SCHEUER is a German author and the recipient of numerous literary awards. He has previously been the University of Duisburg-Essen's Poet in Residence and the University of Bonn's Thomas Kling Poetry Lecturer. Scheuer's 2009 novel *Überm Rauschen* was shortlisted for the German Book Prize and was chosen as Cologne's Book for the City for 2010.

NORBERT SCHEUER

THE LANGUAGE OF BIRDS

Translated by Stephen Brown

First published in English in 2018 by
HAUS PUBLISHING LTD
4 Cinnamon Row
London SW11 3TW

First published in German as *Die Sprache der Vögel* by Norbert Scheuer
Copyright © Verlag C.H.Beck oHG, München 2015

Translation copyright © 2018 Stephen Brown

A CIP catalogue record for this book is available from the British Library

ISBN: 978-1-910376-63-8
eISBN: 978-1-910376-66-9

Illustrations by Erasmus Scheuer

Typeset by MacGuru Ltd

Printed in the UK by TJ International

The translation of this work was supported by a grant from the Goethe-
Institut which is funded by the German Ministry of Foreign Affairs.

GOETHE
INSTITUT

For Elvira

My ancestor Ambrosius Arimond believed that all the birds on our earth possessed a single common language. His entire life he devoted himself to deciphering their songs, a world of magical sounding notes, signs and meanings. For Ambrosius, each species of bird and its song formed a character in a cryptic alphabet. He is said to have recorded the birdsongs in a script of his own devising. The birds' flight silhouettes, which are characteristic of each species, formed the grammar of this language, the sky its parchment of lapis lazuli blue, circling right around the globe and reaching up to the stratosphere, where swifts made love on the wing. His research trips led the young Ambrosius almost everywhere: it is said that in 1776 he crossed the Alps, reached Venice, sailed from there across the eastern Mediterranean, followed the Silk Road as far as Acre, the ancient city of Ptolemais, journeyed onwards into Palestine, joining a caravan across the deserts, along the Euphrates, heading still further eastwards, over remote high mountains, through Persia into what is today Afghanistan. My father often told us stories about Ambrosius, Ambrosius whose notes had for the most part been lost in the Napoleonic Wars, only a few yellowed sheets of parchment were said to lie in an old wooden box in a barn somewhere, handwritten pages, on which he had chronicled his trip through Persia. Ambrosius made his way back to our village eventually and told stories of unknown species of bird, of human beings with zephyr souls, who floated out from the peaks of the Hindu Kush high above the land on a sea of air in ornithopters and kites they had built themselves. I do not know what in these stories is true or whether my father himself believed in them, but he loved to tell us about them. Beyond the Hindu Kush lies the Land of the Birds, he said, there are probably more species of bird there than in the whole of Europe, more than in the whole of the west, on account of the sky's matchless blue.

Magpies flap over the dusty runway. The Asian species has a thin, shiny, greenish hem on its wings and long bronzed tail feathers. It is a touch larger than our native species (*Pica pica germanica*). There are supposed to be five distinct sub-species here. I last saw magpies in Lüneberg in the barracks compound, perched cawing in the crown of an aspen tree, while we sat in a classroom preparing for our deployment to Afghanistan.

The magpies are squabbling over a chick, which they have probably stolen from a nest. They fly up, their wings swirling in the glaring light. As they tear at the tiny animal, their black-white pinions flash dumbfounding beauty, then, cackling, they strut their bobbing walk like aldermen.

I pull on my flak jacket, shoulder my rucksack and march with my comrades past the high barricades of barbed wire. The sun is blazing. My helmet slips on my sweat-drenched forehead. All around shimmers in fantastical shades of brown. Powdery dust the colour of finely ground eggshells, brown rock and the brown of reddish stones, squat bushes, trees like tamarisks, their needles gleaming in pastel colours, tiny grains of sand that cling to my lips and eyebrows. Dazzled, I pinch my eyes shut and then quickly open them again. The magpies have disappeared. For them there are no fences, no barriers.

As our bus takes us from the airfield to our camp and I gaze curiously through the tinted glass at the bustle of the city, I ask myself where the magpies here build their nests. Recognising them here is a comforting reminder of home.

Evening in the camp, still in a makeshift tent, I write a letter to Jan. We've been friends since we were boys, but we've never written letters to each other. Why should we write when we've always been able to meet and talk? Since our accident Jan doesn't speak any more, at least not anything you could describe as speech, he babbles a confused mess of strange, terrifying noises no one can understand – even his mother Odette can't begin to decipher it. Often, as she listens to him like this, she is helpless, and the doctors say only that Jan has suffered an irreversible brain injury. The bones of his skull were smashed in the accident and pressed into his brain. His left eye is damaged. He can no longer remember anything. I don't know if Jan understands what I'm writing to him from Afghanistan, but I refuse to believe that everything is buried in his brain, all the thoughts and experiences we shared. I want to preserve Jan in my memory as he was before our accident. After graduating from school we planned on studying, I wanted to travel, to learn the language of birds, and Jan was to accompany me on my journeys. We fantasised and we laughed about it, because we knew how crazy it all was, no more than a dream.

I try to explain to Jan why I went into the army and became a combat medic and how it is I volunteered for the mission to Afghanistan. I describe my surroundings out here, report back on my comrades, the people I live with in the camp, I tell him about the lake near to the camp and about all the birds I've watched so far.

After the accident I lived for months as if in a vacuum, waiting. My entire life had become meaningless, I lay brooding in bed or wandering aimlessly, nothing interested me any more. I didn't want to talk about what had happened, not even to Theresa. I had the feeling I would lose her too, but I couldn't do anything to stop it. I had no desire for all the studying I had originally planned, but I made no effort to get a job or an apprenticeship either. I argued with my mother frequently, tried to persuade her that there was no value in beginning something new, as I would be drafted into the military soon regardless.

Our camp is an enclosed settlement, with tent accommodation, containers for sleeping and for offices, a bar, a pizzeria, a shopping mall and a post office. There's even a small chapel. Soldiers from four nations are stationed here. As I arrive the camp already seems completely overcrowded, with new contingents arriving every month.

On the first day I complete the necessary formalities with the other new arrivals. An officer points out the safety regulations and tells us about bomb attacks, rockets are fired from the jagged highlands into the camp several times a week, though they rarely cause any casualties, they land in the area outside the camp. On our tour other soldiers greet us, perched on folding chairs outside their container-dormitories, listening to music under camouflage nets stretched out against the sun. Almost the entire surface of the camp has been tarmacked to prevent the spread of the annoying desert mice. In the afternoon we have our photos taken for our security IDs, no one is allowed to stay in the camp without an ID. In my security photo I have cropped hair – almost every man in the camp wears his hair short and his beard long. At first I don't recognise myself in the photo, I'm terrified, I think I've changed completely. But then I see the little bumps on the bridge of my nose. When I was a child I ran into a glass door and broke my nose.

I find a feather on our tour of the camp. I stroke it smooth and place it in my notebook – the first feather I've found here. There are a lot of species I don't know in this country. This bird must be roughly the size of a tit. The intensity of the sun's rays has bleached the feather out.

Back home it's Easter. Theresa says it's been snowing again in the Eifel since Good Friday. She called me out of the blue yesterday. While we were speaking on the phone she was sat on the train to Gerolstein. I haven't spoken to Theresa for a long time, so I was happy to hear her voice. She was telling me that she'd been in Kall to visit Jan. Afterwards she waited for her train in the café at the supermarket. My mother, who's gone back to working as a waitress there, gave her my number. Theresa talked about Jan and her work on a stud farm near a maar. She always wanted to become a groom, she loves horses. At some point in her journey we lost the connection.

Ambrosius describes five species of magpie that he observed on his travels through Afghanistan, distinguishable by the ornamentation of their plumage, by the colour of their beaks and tails and by size. Magpies are members of the crow family and are, in fact, songbirds, even if their loud cawing and chattering isn't necessarily thought of as song. They have colonised almost the entire globe. One magpie is said to bring good fortune, a second one, bad. Pliny the Elder had a high regard for these birds' intelligence. He thought that they took pleasure in uttering certain words, not just that they learned them, but that they loved them, took great pains secretly considering how to use them and could not hide how much this absorbed them. It was a proven fact that magpies would die if they were defeated by the difficulty of a word. When I was twelve I raised a magpie that had fallen from its nest. I fed it every morning before I went to school, soon I had its trust, it would sit itself on my shoulder, plucking at my earlobe and accompanying me on my walks.

In the evening after I have recorded my experiences in my diary, I try to draw the magpies I watched at the airfield. Many ornithologists photograph the birds they watch. But photographs would make me lose the memory of what I have seen. I draw the magpie and think of Theresa.

Magpie (*Pica pica bactriana*)

Theresa and Bruni led the horses out on to the paddock, mucked out the stables and then drove the old Fendt tractor to the field by the maar to repair the fences. It was astonishing how many things had broken over the winter. Theresa had hoped the winter was finally over, but it had frozen again overnight. The farm owner had told them after breakfast that they had to repair the fences. Kessler was a short, smooth-headed old man with a triangular, wrinkled face and thick eyebrows. Bruni knew what to do, she'd been on the farm for a couple of years already. Before she came to the Eifel she had worked as a groom on Baltrum. She'd ridden horses with kids along the beach in the summer but in the winter she couldn't stand the boredom of the island, a place where everything was so easy to understand that the streets didn't even have names. When she read Kessler's advert in an equestrian newspaper, she packed her bags and made the trip. The Kessler farm would be signed over to her in a few years, she told Theresa. Kessler and his wife had promised that she could take over the farm and would only have to pay them a little rent. 'We're old. We're not going to be working much longer,' Kessler had said to her, and his wife had nodded her rumpled, thin face. Bruni was naïve and believed everything the Kesslers told her. She even persuaded herself that the young vet who cared for the horses at the farm was interested in her.

They worked the afternoon down on the shore of the maar. An icy wind swept over the water. It darkened and began to snow. Theresa was wearing Paul's parka over a thick knitted jumper, but she had no work gloves. She pulled the wire tight with aching hands and Bruni hammered the staples into the stakes. Theresa looked out over the maar: a seething mass of birds rose up and then landed again. Whenever she saw birds, Theresa thought of Paul, Paul who had been interested in everything that flew since he was a small boy. Bruni talked incessantly, she was incapable of quiet, even while they worked. She talked about how she would ride out to the maar with the holiday kids in the summer, how they would swim there and lie in the sun all day. Then she started on the vet, what a good-looking guy he was actually and that he had had his eye on her ever since he had taken over the practice from old Dr Langrich a year ago. 'You really don't know him at all,' she said. The new vet had not been working long in the Eifel. He came from somewhere near the Baltic coast. When he visited the farm Bruni ran around after him like a little schoolgirl. She daydreamed about him constantly.

They tensioned another length of wire. Working with the wire had put cracks in Theresa's reddened palms. Every time they began to heal, the wounds would break open again.

As the snowfall thickened, they finished their work, loaded up the tools and drove back on dirt tracks to the farm. The headlights went out for minutes at a time because of a loose connection, and then they were driving blind on the jarring tracks. As the tractor had no windscreen the snow slapped them in the face. At the farm they fed and groomed the horses. People from the city had booked to come the next day, to inspect the premises and perhaps stable their horses there.

Sunday 20 April 2003

Tomorrow is my twenty-fourth birthday, but I won't have time to cele-brate, I won't even have time to make my notes. I'm on ambulance duty the whole day and taking part in a meeting about the mobile medical unit (BAT) in the evening. I haven't even mentioned my birthday to my dorm-mates Sergei and Julian, I'd be embarrassed to celebrate it. I don't know why that is. I can't settle my mind, I'm finding it hard to have a clear thought. I have no idea where this unease is coming from. Perhaps it's fear. I'm hot all the time. I can't drink as much as I'm losing in sweat. Mother and Sabine will call tomorrow, probably. Where is my sister living and what is she doing? After Father died she perched herself near the Zingsheim motorway bridge almost every evening, staring up at the pillars. She sat on the grass, took drugs and covered her ears because she couldn't bear the cries of the falcons that nested there, high up. She heard them, even though falcons are silent in the darkness. Then at some point it was as if she disappeared off the face of the earth, and I was glad that at least she wouldn't have to go to that fucking bridge any more.

Once, in the old days, I cycled with Dad into the Boletal to the limestone quarry, I was allowed to sit on the crossbar. 'We're flying!' I shouted. Dad called out the names of the songbirds as they flew past us, imitated their trills, I would soon learn to do it too. A pair of eagle owls were nesting in the quarry. We heard their whispering wing beats.

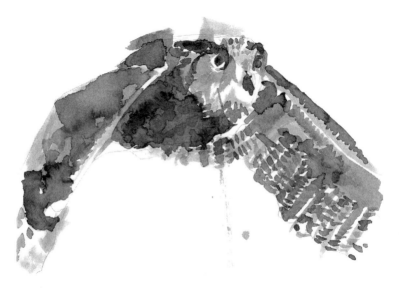

Eagle owl (*Bubo bubo*)

Tuesday 22 April 2003

For the first time, after my shift, I climb up to the lookout, a wooden tower in the centre of the camp. I hope that from there I will see the lake I noticed on our way to the camp. The lake shimmers a turquoise green, perhaps it's caused by dissolved salts, other minerals and tiny crabs. It's a long way from the dusty track that leads from the city to the camp. From the tower I look out over our camp, at the offices and sleeping quarters in containers, at the protective wall of cuboid steel cages full of rocks, stacked on top of each other. Outside this rampart runs a strip of land enclosed by a fence crowned with barbed wire. Afghan guardposts and our own soldiers watch over the camp. Beyond the fence I can make out low bushes, steppe grass, fallow fields, sand dunes with fine dust swirling over them. In the far distance flocks of birds move over the lake like rags swaying gently in the wind. Many of these birds are probably strangers in this country, just as we are. They've flown thousands of kilometres to rest here. The lake is about five kilometres away in a northwesterly direction. I could get there on foot in about an hour. I resolve to go at the next opportunity. I want to watch the birds, I hope I can discover species unknown to me. Even though it's forbidden to leave the camp without express permission, I absolutely want to sit on that shore.

I often put off writing my notes until the following day. I lie in bed, thinking of the birds I've seen. I often fall asleep like that. It's a good way of not getting trapped in my thoughts.

In the spring of 2004, when Helena suddenly fell seriously ill, Ignatz moved her bed into the piano room next to the kitchen so that she wouldn't have to climb down the steep staircase from her bedroom to the kitchen and living room. An old stone house was no place for the sick. They had bought the house on the cheap from the mining company when they'd moved to Kall thirty years ago. They had liked it immediately, and later their children were born and raised there.

From her bed Helena looked out across a large field. In the summer the horses had cropped the grass around the tall thistles, creating small islands of wild teasel, bee thistle and creeping thistle. Beyond the meadow stood a pine forest, which hid the waste pools and pumping basins of the old lead mine that adjoined a military training ground, a wilderness barred to the public because of the danger of the old mining tunnels collapsing. Helena had lain in bed the whole summer. On some days she simply slept or watched the thistle seeds wafting and glittering over the meadow. Helena asked herself what Ignatz would do when she was no longer here. She had always assumed that he couldn't live without her. She thought about her affair with Leo, their secret meetings. She wondered whether, if she must die, she would regret having seen Leo so rarely. She had written to him that they could no longer meet. It was impossible for her in her current situation to be with him in a hotel room in the city. She fell asleep, and when she woke again, silvery thistle seeds were floating through the window into the room, some of their filigree forms caught on the bedcover. Helena blew them back into the air. She imagined sailing like a seed parachute. Once, as she woke again, a chaffinch flew into the room and settled on a key of the piano, fluttered upwards, then landed back down, chirping as it did so. She was waiting for Ignatz. He had gone to the supermarket to do the shopping for the weekend. After that, she had an appointment at the hospital.

Helena was standing at the front door when Ignatz came home. She was wearing a wig and had put on lipstick. Ignatz parked at the entrance to the garage, got out of the car, looked at her adoringly and took her in his arms. He was much taller than she was, had long grey hair and wore a small silver earring. When they first met, he had been studying law in Bonn, but after the first state examination he abandoned his studies and became a social worker. They moved to Kall, where he ran a residential project for young people with behavioural issues. Helena had worked there as a teacher before she fell ill.

'You look pretty,' Ignatz said. She didn't exactly believe him, but it didn't matter. His eyes gleamed; they were the most beautiful thing about him. They emptied the boot of the car together. Ignatz put the baskets into the small storeroom next to the garage. They put the meat in the fridge. They didn't have time for a coffee; they had to go straight out again. Ignatz always took her to the clinic. He didn't want her to take the train.

During the journey she laid her hand on his leg. Ignatz was dressed, as always, like a student: his jeans were faded and his shirt hung out over his trousers. He talked about the residential unit. The young people he looked after had no apprenticeships, could find no jobs and had drug problems as well. One girl had cut her own arm and had nearly bled to death. 'Mara only hurts herself so that she won't feel anything else any more,' said Ignatz.

Before her illness, it was Helena who had driven the car. Ignatz would look out of the window and play the blues on his mouth organ; she missed that now, as she missed many other things that had been mere trivialities to her before. She would never explain her relationship with Leo to Ignatz. Helena closed her eyes, listened to the music on the radio, on the news they were forecasting heavy rain and hurricane winds for the evening. She thought of the thistle seeds, scattered to all points of the compass by the storm.

Ignatz held her hand as they walked across the car park. 'That young man is up there again,' she said. Every time they were heading into the hospital, he was standing there at a window on the fifth floor, looking down at the car park. Ignatz could not stay this time, he had to go back to work.

Helena woke up in the treatment room hours after her therapy. She asked the nurse about the test results, discovered that the doctor had actually already gone home, but it was probably all fine, otherwise he would have spoken to her. The visitor's café was being cleaned. Helena sat herself down on a chair in the foyer. Ignatz wasn't answering his phone. A woman was sitting at reception, but Helena could see nothing except her mass of hair. It had gone dark outside in the meantime. Patients stood under a canopy and smoked. Visitors walked along the long corridor to the lifts. It had begun to rain. The face of the receptionist emerged from behind the counter to give information to a man who had just entered, soaking wet. Helena flicked through a glossy magazine. A young man was standing in front of her, he was wearing a military uniform and had a stack of paper in his hands. He was definitely not a former pupil of hers, she knew that. Perhaps he was one of Ignatz's kids. Now it came to her. 'Julian?' He nodded and smiled shyly, she saw his dimple and his thin, severe lips, his eyes like deep-blue marbles, she'd recognised him by his eyes. You could hardly believe how children change, she thought.

'How is your husband?' asked Julian. At just that moment, her phone rang. 'This is him now,' she said. 'Say hello to him from me please,' said Julian and took a few steps back. As she spoke to Ignatz she could hear the background noise of the residential unit, shouts and hysterical screams. Ignatz left the room, presumably he was now standing in the corridor. 'How are you, darling? Do you have your results?' 'I don't know anything, and I'm not going to learn anything more today either,' she answered. 'I'll fetch you as soon as I'm done. You wouldn't believe the scene here. I've been neglecting the children for too long.' Ignatz sounded strained. 'There's a terrible storm raging here. It's ripped the roof off the shed and bits of it have landed on our car.' 'No, really? Then I can come home on the train,' she suggested. 'No, no, you're not doing that.' 'But I feel better than I have in such a long time. I've met Julian here,' she said, to change the subject. Ignatz remembered him instantly. 'Could you give him the phone please?' She called Julian over and held out the phone to him. 'I always wanted to write to you, but I never got around to it,' Julian apologised. He said that he'd been in Afghanistan, had been visiting a comrade in the hospital. Then Ignatz spoke, and Julian listened carefully. 'Of course, I'd be pleased to do that,' he said eventually. Julian gave the phone back to her. 'Fine. I'll get a lift with Julian.' She had no desire to argue. 'I love you,' whispered Ignatz. 'And I you,' she replied. She stowed her phone back in her handbag.

Outside it stormed, the whistling wind swirled wet leaves and scraps of paper through the air, a gust swept an umbrella across the car park and tangled it in the crown of a plane tree. Helena could not remember ever experiencing a storm like this before. As Julian opened the door of his old Mercedes, the stack of papers fell out of his hand. Some of them landed in a puddle; others swirled through the air. Julian crouched down in front of the car gathering up the wet pages, asked Helena to stay where she was and then ran after the remaining pages. As they sat themselves in the car, it began to hail. The sheets were lying on Helena's lap. They were half torn and soaked through, the ink had run. 'What is this?' she asked. 'A comrade, the one I was visiting in the hospital, he wrote it.' They drove slowly through the city on a carpet of hailstones, then onwards through the suburban estates and business parks. Felled trees lay on the country road, the underpass was flooded, cars were stuck fast under the bridge, a driver had climbed on to the roof of his car. They had to turn around and take another route. It was unnerving for Helena, and yet she felt in some reckless way happy, she was not afraid, no matter what might happen to her. 'I feel bad putting you through all this on my account,' she said. 'I'm happy to do it. I have no plans anyway. Your husband helped me a lot in the past.' 'Do you have a girlfriend?' Helena wanted to know. 'No.' 'Will you tell me about Afghanistan?' 'There's not much point telling someone about it if they haven't been there.' Now his voice sounded like the voice of a small stubborn boy. She was still holding the sodden manuscript on her lap. 'I'd very much like to read this,' she said. Julian got out of the car and lifted the barrier for the military road. They drove on in silence, through the old military base, at the edge of which stood Helena's house. She had never driven down this road, had forbidden her children from playing here. Leaves and twigs torn from the trees dropped on to the windscreen. 'I thought this road was closed,' she said. 'Strictly speaking, it is. But not today and not for us,' Julian answered. The wheels rolled slowly over the well-worn furrows of the tank road. The road rose gently, led them deeper into a bizarre landscape of heaps of gravel and lead-grey sand, into an ancient forest of birch and pine. 'Isn't it dangerous here?' she asked. 'Don't worry. I'll get you home safe.' The storm had subsided, the sky had cleared, the stars were shining. Moonlight fell on the lake of wastewater from the mine. The dark forms of birds took off and whirred low over the water; Helena heard what must have been the cries of terns. They had reached a plateau, where the winding tower jutted into the sky. 'You get an amazing view from up there,' Julian said. 'Shall we go up?' 'I don't know if I'd make it.' 'Let's just try,' he encouraged her. They strode out through the tall wet grass. The door to the tower was locked. 'I'm sorry. I promised you too much. You used to be able to just walk in, there were no locked doors.' 'I don't think I would have made it up there anyway.' As they plodded back to the car through the dripping grass, their hands touched for a moment. She felt dizzy. 'What's wrong?' asked Julian. 'Oh, it's the treatment, it takes it out of me, I've probably over-exerted myself.' 'Do you need to hold on to me?' 'No, no. Let's just wait a bit.' Then everything was spinning around her and she lost consciousness.

When she came to she was laid out comfortably reclining on the passenger seat. Julian had taken off her damp shoes and stockings and wrapped her feet in a warm blanket. They drove on slowly. The smell of withered leaves wafted in through the open window. She felt as if the journey would never end, perhaps because they were moving at walking pace through a foreign landscape. The road finally ended at a steep slope. They sat next to each other without speaking and looked at the scarp walls of a volcanic crater. The moon was shining brightly. In the rock opposite Helena could make out caves, in which humans had lived thousands of years before. The water of the lake reflected the rock faces in the valley bottom. At some point, Helena fell asleep. When she woke, it was getting light, the first birds were singing. Little by little more and more voices blended into the concert. Helena could see out beyond the territory of the mineworks as far as the city, where Leo lived with his family. She had never told anyone about Leo. 'The birdsong is most beautiful in the morning,' she said. 'In Afghanistan, my comrade always wanted to go to this lake, it was a couple of kilometres from our camp, to watch the birds there,' said Julian. 'He was obsessed with it, like there was something special there for him to discover.'

In the daytime we newcomers are assigned to ward duties. Every day the ambulance brings patients into the camp's emergency medical centre. On top of that we have our outpatient consulting hours for the locals. Life in the camp is even more monotonous than in barracks back home. Wake up, breakfast, clean dorm, work assignments, training, advanced training, lunch break, medical duties, clocking off, supper, peace.

On top of that, along with the boring training, we listen to talks about the geography and flora and fauna of the country.

Dr Nogge, an old academic with a grey beard, who was the director of the Kabul Zoo before the war, lectures on Afghanistan. From a zoological point of view, he says, it's one of the most interesting countries on earth, with many diverse habitats, an untamed land, which combines the Palearctic (Eurasian) and Oriental (India). The little dot of his laser pointer jitters over a topographic map, indicating the Hindu Kush and its surrounding mountains. Around them stretches a broad belt of steppe and desert. Dr Nogge shows us photos of the vast mountains, which until now I have seen only in the distance. They stand over 7,000 metres in height. I imagine Ambrosius more than two hundred years ago, exploring the mountains on a mule, his pack mule with his tightly fastened luggage following behind him. In those days, it seems, Afghanistan was a thriving, peaceful Arcadia. I think of Ambrosius's scant notes, remember his account of a turquoise lake where he made camp and watched the birds. In the last few years birds had completely vanished from my sight, as if they'd retreated into invisible caverns in the air.

'Afghanistan is an arid land with no direct access to the sea,' I hear Dr Nogge announcing. 'In the southwest, on the border with Iran, we find a plain without an outlet, with a vast inland sea, fed by the Helmand river, called Hamun-e Puzak. To the northeast the Hindu Kush joins up with the Pamir Mountains and forms the Central Asian watershed.' Next to me, Sergei yawns. This doesn't interest him. He fetches his

Rubik's Cube out of his bag and spins it under the desk. Yesterday he told me that by doing this he can forget everything. Perhaps life depends on this: finding something that makes everything else fade into oblivion. 'In the east of Afghanistan, in Nuristan, there are extensive forests of cedar and pine. Here, as everywhere in this country, we find an exceptional diversity of species.' Dr Nogge shows us photos of snow leopards, gazelles, foxes, brown bears, flocks of pink flamingos, Asian house martins, crimson-winged finches, white-capped redstarts, citrine wagtails, black-necked cranes and Siberian cranes. 'Many of these birds are resting here on lakes and reservoirs during their migrations to their winter habitats. In the spring they come from central Asia, crossing the 3,000-metre-high Salang Pass, flying between vast mountain chains, which move closer and closer together to form a vast funnel. The resulting flow of air through the pass pulls the birds along, as if in an air duct, high over the snow-covered mountains.'

I call my mother, I get through to her at work. She doesn't have much time because late afternoon is always very busy at the café in the supermarket. She walks with her mobile from the counter into the kitchen so we can talk for a couple of minutes in peace. In the background I hear an announcement from the shopping mall. Mother complains that I'm only calling her now and that she's heard nothing from me in months. She gripes that I call her so infrequently, but when I do telephone she has no time to talk to me. I don't know what we're supposed to talk about. She asks me why I've gone to this country. Every time she watches the news, she's scared, she's afraid that something has happened to me. I ask after Jan. Mother says that Odette was with him in the supermarket, he was pulling hideous faces, it was depressing to see him like that. One of her colleagues calls my mother, she has to come out and serve immediately, there are bread rolls to be taken out of the automated oven, customers are waiting for their coffee.

Mother told me that Theresa was in the café with a stocky, short-haired female friend. The pair of them stank of the stables, they had shit on their boots and were filthy all over. Theresa was wearing my old parka and a baggy woollen jumper. She'd got skinny and looked scruffy. While Theresa was visiting Jan at home, her dreadful friend had lounged about in the café, surreptitiously fetching a bottle from her rucksack and tipping something from it into her coffee. Eventually she fell asleep in one of the club armchairs, drunk. She had piercings in her lips and eyebrows. My mother cannot stand women with piercings. When Theresa returned, she had a row with her friend, and then at some point they walked off to the railway station.

At night, when the rockets fly over the camp, the whistling noise wakes me up.

Friday 25 April 2003

After ten days in a makeshift tent, I move with Julian and Sergei into a dorm container near to the helicopter landing pad, with well-sprung camp beds and metal lockers. Our predecessors have scratched their names on to the doors of the lockers. The head of my bed is under a dust-covered window. If I tilt my head back, the watery, thin cirrostratus drift over me, the sky is vast and endless. In the far distance a booted eagle circles, letting the updrafts carry it into the heights, until is no longer visible.

In my first year of secondary school I wrote an essay about birds. My father had just recently told us about Ambrosius. Our teacher placed her chair up on her desk. Whenever she especially liked an essay, the pupil had to climb up on to her desk, sit down on the chair and read out their story from up there. My classmates laughed at my story, our teacher had to tell them to behave. Jan liked my essay, even though he had no interest in birds. We became friends after that.

I lie on my cot, listening to my comrades fooling around, Sergei's nasal twang, his pleasant Slavic accent. He has a small operation scar above his lips, his nose is a little crooked. He and Julian have resounding laughs, I like to listen to them, they're friendly to me, I've been lucky with my barrack mates. When Julian speaks he takes care to avoid even one grammatical error, he talks about the most banal things as if he were delivering a scientific paper. Now they're laughing again, and Sergei is circling his palm on the close-cropped whorl of hair on the back of his head. He always does that when he's considering something, he smiles as he does it. I close my eyes, listening contentedly to their chatter and laughter.

In 1789 Ambrosius is said to have returned from Afghanistan, in what was then the Pashtun Empire, to the Eifel, to have lived once again in our village and worked on his writing about bird language. He would sit in front of his cottage by the river wearing a broad-sleeved, collarless shirt and a turban. It is said that he looked like a being from another world, telling stories of the distant lands he had visited. Perhaps that's why so many people moved away from our village and their descendants now live all over the world. My father said that Ambrosius spent almost three years travelling on foot to Afghanistan, following the route of the old Silk Road, through lands that the people of village had never heard of before, until eventually he reached Persia, Turkmenistan and the fabled kingdom of Bactria, where it was said the birds could speak. He lived in this country for several years before he returned home again – but he didn't stay very long. Father said Ambrosius was a clever man, who had attended the grammar school at the Steinfeld Abbey as a child and learned to read and write there. But he was never able to tolerate living in one place for long, on account of which he had left the monastery, his home village and his country to tramp around the world. After living a few more years in the village he travelled to Italy with Napoleon's army. Supposedly he had worked with Jean-François Champollion unlocking the mystery of Egyptian hieroglyphics. Years later he took part in the campaign against Russia. He had hoped he might travel from Russia through Kurdistan back to Afghanistan to continue his study of the birds there. But at the gates of Moscow the harsh Russian winter took the hitherto triumphant French army by surprise. The cold foiled all of Napoleon's plans for conquest; thousands of soldiers, Ambrosius amongst them, dragged themselves back to their homelands along ice-bound roads through the endless expanses of Russia. Their route was littered with frozen men, jettisoned booty, abandoned carriages and slaughtered draught animals. In order not to freeze to death like so many of his comrades, Ambrosius is said to have killed his horse and gutted it; he ate parts of the heart and liver before crawling into the warmth of the animal's corpse along with his kitbag, where he kept his notes, correspondence and diary. In this way he survived the ice-cold night, only to be taken prisoner the next morning by Cossacks. He left his kitbag, which contained almost all his writings, in the belly of the animal. Thus his notes on the language of birds were lost. When Ambrosius eventually returned from captivity to our little village he was a confused and broken man.

Saturday 26 April 2003

During a break I sit on the steps of the medical container and watch two collared doves (*Streptopelia decaocto*), which have ventured into the camp and are perched about five metres from me on the gravel path. Their plumage is beige, and they peer mildly out through intelligent, reddish eyes, as if I'm really not there at all. It pleases me to see how they have occupied our camp. Collared doves originally ranged from Turkey to Japan, but since the beginning of the twentieth century they have become restless world travellers, quickly adapting to every new environment. Like all birds, they have their own geography, to them the arbitrary lines of our borders mean nothing. The doves are so funny, walking around me, picking up little stones in their beaks. I think of home, of the mating pair of doves who bred in the rowan tree in our garden. They may very well still be nesting there. As a child, my sister was so frightened by their cooing that one morning she stood by my bed whimpering in fear.

I use a grained paper, a little thicker than copier paper, to draw the outline of the dove. I cross-hatch the darker parts of the plumage and shadows with my pencil, then mark where the plumage shines. I brew up an extremely strong coffee – *c.* four to five spoons of coffee to half a cup of water – in our little aluminium espresso maker. Sergei once drank my watercolour-coffee by mistake and declared: Finally some proper coffee! Not like the watery muck in the canteen. With my brush I fish out the coffee pigment that has sunk to the bottom and use it first of all to paint the dark details. After that I let the first layer dry, which doesn't take long in this intense heat. By letting it dry I can achieve distinct areas of varying light and dark. To make the darker parts, I have to paint the areas several times, leaving them to dry each time before I paint the almost white plumage of my dove. I apply lighter and lighter coats in sequence. Each coat has to dry out before I can paint the next. So, depending on the bird, I may need as many as seven rounds (two hours) and at least three (forty-five minutes). The only corrections I can make are to lighten the already dried layers with water, but doing so usually spoils the paper. By the time I've completed a bird, the wetness has corrugated the sheet. I lay the finished drawing between books to press it. Julian has lent me weighty tomes on military strategy and tactics for this purpose – including *Reibert: The Handbook for German Soldiers*. When the drawings have dried, they smell sourly of coffee, a peculiar scent.

Collared dove (*Streptopelia decaocto*)

By the time Helena woke up, Ignatz had long since gone to work. She had just had her breakfast when he called her to ask how she was. She had eaten well and felt better. Ignatz said over the phone that he wanted to pick up the car after work from the garage on the industrial estate. All the damage caused by the storm had finally been repaired. While they were speaking, maple leaves in the garden were spiralling on to the meadow, the gossamer threads of orb-weaver spiders linked solitary twigs. Helena remembered the pages of manuscript Julian had given her. Did they really come from Paul? Helena believed she had recognised Paul in the young man who had been standing at the hospital window. The bundle of sheets of paper she pulled out of her handbag felt like a damp rag. Now that she looked more closely at the stuck-together pages, she was sure of it, they were Paul's. Back then it had taken her a while before she could decipher his scrawling hand. Paul had been a withdrawn, gangling boy who sat in the back row by the window and spent the lessons beadily watching the birds in the school gardens and producing small drawings of them. She'd let him get on with it, he wasn't disturbing the class at all. When Paul was watching the birds he seemed to become absolutely calm and at the same time more attentive. If she asked him a question, he invariably had an answer to hand, sometimes a peculiar one, but always an answer. She remembered an accident in Paul's family, and she thought of his mother, who she had seen from time to time in the café at the supermarket, a beautiful woman, a little too dolled-up for Helena's taste. She didn't live in the area any longer. She'd remarried and had recently moved in with her new husband in the north.

Julian had said he couldn't take the notes back with him to Afghanistan. Perhaps he originally wanted to give them to Paul's mother, but he hadn't seen her. Helena was curious, she wanted to begin reading straight away, but she had to dry the pages first. So she took the pages upstairs to what had been their marital bedroom. Since she'd moved downstairs, it had been cleared completely, save for one tall-stemmed vase standing alone in a corner under the slope of the roof. Dried-out flowers stood in the vase, flowers Ignatz had brought for her one day. The room smelled musty, it hadn't been aired for so long. From the large dormer window you could look out over the fields as far as the treetops beyond. The sun shone, and the autumn colours stepped forward in all their subtlety, the pines at the edge of the woods exhaled pollen. Helena laid the manuscript out on the floorboards, one sheet next to another, as if she were assembling a mosaic of words.

Paul had recorded his observations of birds in notes like a diary. On some pages the dates were no longer legible. She came across stories from Kall and stories of a certain Ambrosius, an ancestor, who had travelled to Persia at the end of the eighteenth century. As Helena carefully laid the damp sheets out on the floor she began to worry that the room might be too small, it wouldn't be able to take all the pages. This thought almost threw her into a panic; she thought that if there wasn't space for all the pages, undiscovered connections between things and ideas would be torn apart. But in the end they did all fit, as if they had been written with exactly that in mind, and one clear spot remained next to the door, enough space for her. She was still sitting there when evening fell and Ignatz came home. She had the feeling that only a few moments had passed.

Sunday 27 April 2003

There are two helicopters in constant readiness on our landing pad. One to transport the wounded, the other to use its on-board weaponry when required to protect the medical response helicopter from the air. The vehicles allocated to our platoon stand in a neat row next to the landing pad: armoured ambulances and transporters, Dingos, which look like tall slender Jeeps. They are completely enclosed for increased protection from bomb attacks; a raised superstructure conceals a station for remote-controlled weaponry. The soft suspension makes them rock like a ship in high seas. When we go out on patrol in a Dingo it's impossible to watch birds.

Most of the time I'm not paying attention to what I'm supposed to be watching, and when I do look at things I notice something else anyway, brown dust, which floats quietly and gracefully like birds, the sight of which seems to change everything.

Tuesday 29 April 2003

Theresa called me today from Daun. She'd gone there shopping with Bruni. She says how exhausting life on the farm is, tells me about her accommodation next to the stables, essentially a horsebox, overstuffed with old furniture and with broken heating. You're not allowed to light the oven for fear of fire. The boss checks up on her every night. Nothing they do is good enough for Kessler's malicious wife. Each evening she walks around the farm with her dogs. The Dalmatians snoop and pry, like spirits in the service of their mistress on her travels, black-spotted dogs with lithe bodies on long scrawny legs. She and Bruni have had to take on the farmhand's work after he disappeared without a trace a few weeks ago. I can hear Bruni's voice in the background. She's calling impatiently, she's moving on. Theresa tells me that Bruni has an old scooter, without which they'd have no possibility of getting away from the farm. The supermarkets in Daun stay open into the evening and there's a bus stop on the country road near the farm, but the last bus leaves at 1800 when they're still at work in the stables. She wants to know how I am, why I haven't been in touch for so long, she worries about me. 'Do you even like talking to me on the phone?' she asks. Her voice trembles. 'I enjoy it,' I answer. Her mobile doesn't work on Kessler's farm, otherwise she'd have called me sooner.

In the summer holidays we went on our bicycles to the maar. It seems an eternity ago. We pitched our little tent in a meadow and made love for the first time. Afterwards Theresa crawled out of the tent and ran down to the shore of the lake. I thought I'd done something wrong. She was crouching on the jetty, crying. When I asked her why she was crying, she answered, 'Because I'm happy.' We jumped into the lake and swam along its edge in the dark until we reached a bank of reeds. I remember her glittering eyes when she laughed. I remember her breathing as she slept next to me in the tent. While I was reading the light of my torch fell on her naked feet. Why do these memories come to me here, when everything is so impossibly far removed and it would be better to forget it all?

Mother was up early to go to work. Every morning, before the supermarket opened, the cakes and bread delivered from the bakery had to be put out on to the shelves and the lumps of dough for rolls shoved into the oven. Everything had to be ready before the first customer arrived. I can hear Mother downstairs in the kitchen, talking on the phone. She's telling her boyfriend about the marten. After Father's funeral, she'd met a new man at the health spa. He'd lost his wife. He called her often in the early mornings, then one time he came to visit her, driving through the night from a small village near Hamburg to the Eifel. He waited for her for hours in the café at the supermarket. My mother sat down with him in her break and he proposed to her.

As I walked into the kitchen in my pyjamas, my mother was still sitting at the kitchen table and talking on the phone. She hadn't done her make-up, and her hair was a mess. Since she got a boyfriend she'd been letting her hair grow again. She was talking about the marten, as if it were a good old friend, though she was afraid of it too. The animal had ignored every bait in the trap for months, choosing instead to massacre our neighbours' Indian Runner ducks, dragging their heads under the bonnet of the car and biting through an ignition cable. Now the marten was caught in the trap, crouched in a steel-wire cage my mother had set at the back of the garage. It had wanted to gorge itself on the raw eggs inside, it had triggered the mechanism and the grille had dropped. The marten had been imprisoned in the cage ever since, its eyes flashing amber in the darkness. Whenever someone stepped into the garage, it jumped about fiercely in the cage and scratched at the bars, hissing. My mother was afraid of it, but now, talking to her boyfriend, she sounded different. I was annoyed at my mother's peculiar way of always pretending to be amused and unconcerned, though the reality was quite different. He's in for a shock, I thought to myself, and left the kitchen. I couldn't stand their loved-up whisperings any longer. In the end my mother demanded that I remove the marten, take it a long way away, so it could never come back. The marten was restless and hungry. It had got used to me feeding it every morning.

Friday 2 May 2003

Hardly a day goes by at camp without me climbing the tower in the evening after I come off duty. I have my binoculars, a water bottle and some books, which I've borrowed for the purpose from the camp library. The library is housed in a small container next to the post office. I've gone back to Emerson and Thoreau. For a long time I devoured solely textbooks of anatomy and emergency medicine for my paramedic training. Now I am reading Thoreau, and I understand it very differently from before, much better, I think. *Both place and time were changed, and I dwelt nearer to those parts of the universe and to those eras in history which had most attracted me. Where I lived was as far off as many a region viewed nightly by astronomers.*

The wooden roof of the lookout tower offers shade, and a cool evening wind blows through the open parapet. The moon glitters on the lake. Perhaps Ambrosius camped by its waters and watched the birds. In recent weeks I've been able to see the lake in passing through the little window of the armoured personnel carrier. I can see neither inflow nor outflow of water – perhaps it is fed by underground springs or by meltwater and rainfall in the spring. It seems to host a great number of different bird species. In countries like Afghanistan, which have no direct access to the sea, inland bodies of water are especially important for birdlife.

Migration has begun. Today I was able to watch a water pipit in its breeding colours right up close on a satellite dish. For days the barn swallows and house martins have been moving north. The weather forecast is promising us rising temperatures and sunshine for the days ahead. Every day I am eavesdropping on bird calls I have never heard before.

Sunday 4 May 2003

A squad of red-fronted serins have taken up residence in the prohibited area. To get to the lake, I'll have to cross the prohibited area once
I've climbed over the Hesco wall. I'm wondering how to get to the
fence safely. I'll have to crawl for metres before I can run onwards,
stooping, under cover of the dyke. The fence has a barbed-wire crown,
a tangle of razor-sharp points. But I don't want to think about that,
I'm just going to enjoy the birds that I see in the camp or out on patrol.
My request to be allowed to look at the plants and animals outside the
camp was rejected on the grounds of military security.

Now the serins are hopping about nervously on the low bushes in
the rocky terrain. Some of the males are courting, enthusiastically performing their songs, letting their wings droop and raising their head
plumage, so that their red foreheads stand out. I don't believe that
birds sing only for the purposes of breeding. There is something in life
greater than us and for which there is no language. Perhaps that's the
reason that birds sing.

Sergei is sitting on one of the aluminium boxes we used to stow our belongings for the journey here. Since we've emptied everything out into our lockers, the boxes serve us as seating and a table. Sergei is short and stocky, has alert, open eyes, which blink nervously from time to time, and he's clever, in an oblivious way. Like many Russian Germans he was born in a small village in Siberia, his parents emigrated to Germany, he struggled at school because he knew hardly any German and made no friends, but he always had his Rubik's Cube. Sergei says that his father was in Afghanistan for five years with the Soviet Army. While he tells us about it, he plays with the Rubik's Cube, just as he did secretly throughout our training and lectures. When he laughs his large protruding ears shake. Because of the short haircuts, many of our comrades look as if they have sticking-out ears. 'We're an army of bat ears,' laughs Sergei. He is married, has small children, calls home often. His voice always sounds sad when he's fooling around with his kids. I sense his longing for home, when he speaks to his wife or asks after his parents, his voice betrays how much he loves his parents. At night he murmurs his wife's name in his sleep. I think he embraces her in his sleep, kisses her, roams the length of her body with his lips and crawls inside her. Sergei has proudly shown me her picture on his laptop, and he has a photo of his family stuck on the inside of his locker door. When he calls his wife I usually leave him alone in the container, sit outside under our awning. Here, for the first time, I consider how I can leave the camp unobserved, to get to the lake. It looks hopeless, the camp is closely guarded and in the prohibited area (the secure zone between the Hesco bastion wall and the perimeter fence) there is an electronic barrier as well. Despite the impossibility of crossing the prohibited area undetected, I lie awake at night sweating and racking my brains as to how I can overcome the obstacles that lie on my way to the lake.

Red-fronted serin (*Serinus pusillus*)

In the spring of 1996 I watched peregrine falcons (*Falco peregrinus*) with my father. They had settled in our area again after a long gap and made their home in an abandoned raven's nest on the top of a concrete pier under the Zingsheim Viaduct. We parked under the motorway bridge at a nearby pathway, took our binoculars from the back seat and clambered up the slope, up past the vast concrete piers to a spot well above them, from where we had a view over the falcon's eyrie. The nest lay unreachably high, at the top of the pier that rose out of the valley, well protected, in a niche on the plinth where the carriageway rested on a thick iron girder. It was an ideal spot for rearing their young. Below in the valley the country road ran towards Münstereifel. Next to the road a stream lined with hawthorn hedge and elder bushes meandered through a meadow. A falcon returned from the hunt. During the breeding season falcons take turns to look for food: first the somewhat smaller male goes out to hunt, then the female. The male announced himself with shrill cries. My father and I were sat in a good position, we could see into the nest with our binoculars. Three young peregrine falcons had only just hatched. They were still covered in their coats of fluffy down. We watched how the falcon plucked at a stricken pigeon and fed small gobbets of flesh to his young. Meanwhile the female had already begun to hunt, for a while she lingered near the bridge and showed us her daredevil aerial stunts before vanishing above the pastures of the limestone mountains. We stayed seated in our spot and watched the young falcons in the nest.

As it was beginning to grow dark, we saw a man running along the side of the road towards the bridge. Once he reached it he disappeared from our view. Then I watched as, with arms outstretched, he flew through the air. Perhaps for a moment I thought, and even he thought, that he was a bird. He must have jumped from the middle of the bridge, at the height of the pier with the falcon's nest. In the months that followed people jumped from the bridge to their deaths again and again, even a girl from another class in my year. No one could explain why she had done it. She was reckoned to be a good pupil, she was pretty and popular with everyone. She was only discovered a few days later, by chance, in the meadow by the little stream. After her suicide they fixed railings to the sides of the bridge.

No one could look down from it into the valley any longer. Some people are drawn by depth. Perhaps they want, just for a moment, to be weightless and free.

The following year my father went to the bridge alone and watched the falcons. I wasn't going with him any more – I was by then at an age when birds no longer interested me. But they were always there regardless, like invisible messengers between human beings.

Tuesday 6 May 2003

I spend almost every evening in the camp bar with Julian and Sergei. We run a table-football tournament there, battling with the French, the Americans and the Poles. Every nation has its own special procedure for preventing sweaty hands slipping on the handles of the rods. One rubs talcum powder on to the wooden handles, another swears by condoms of various colours pulled over the grips. Whoever loses has to crawl under the table, scrawl their emblem on the underside of the football field and drink a mixture of beer and schnapps. Some of our comrades end up so drunk they can't get out from under the table unaided. A great quantity of schnapps is drunk clandestinely, even though excessive alcohol consumption is forbidden and can even lead to you being repatriated.

As we are lying in our beds tonight, Julian tells us about a woman he encountered at a nightclub in Cologne and who he's not been able to forget since. He'd never before seen a woman so intensely charismatic, he says, the kind of woman that without question you meet only once in your life. We lie in the darkness, listening eagerly. Julian says that he doesn't even know her name, he didn't even speak with her much. She looked at him, he walked over to her and then, after they left the club, they drove through the night along a country road. The woman took off her shoes and stockings first, laughed loudly, then unbuttoned her blouse and slipped it off, and finally her bra. By now she couldn't stop laughing, she wound down the window and threw her shoes, her clothes and anything she found in the car out of the window, even his CDs, which were sitting in the glove compartment. After they had driven over a motorway bridge, Julian stopped at the side of the road. She laughed like a maniac, he said, and then they made love. Afterwards she got out of the car, ran barefoot and naked across the grass and then was lost in the darkness. He called out for her and waited until it grew light. But she had disappeared. When he got back to barracks, late, he was given a reprimand and confined to base for three weekends. And though he went back to that club many times, he never saw the woman again.

Peregrine falcon (*Falco peregrinus*)

Julian doesn't get any phone calls. No one writes him letters or emails. He never mentions his family. One time he actually said that he didn't have any parents, he came into the world at fifteen years old.

Wednesday 7 May 2003

Today in my lunch break I watched Dead Sea sparrows (*Passer moabit-icus*). They take dust baths in front of the medical tent. I recognise the adult males by their sombre, ash-grey heads and the white spot under their cheeks. The females are mouse grey on the head and neck, rust brown and dirty yellow on the back. It seems as if the birds want to wear this country's many shades of brown in their feathers. They perch on the rolls of wire, a jumble of squeaking and squawking noises, chatter followed by quiet piping crystalline notes. Perhaps for these sparrows there is no distinction between language and melody. As they fly up they spin dust colours into the sky.

They are nesting in the wreckage of a Russian tank, not so far away from the helicopter landing pad. I count nine males there. They have made their breeding sites underneath the mechanism of the gun turret, in the hatches and the muzzles of the cannon. The males entice the females with unceasing high chirruping notes. When a female alights on the boundary wall, one male approaches with drooping, quivering wings, raised head and fanned tail. The female adopts a threatening posture nonetheless and then takes flight, whereupon the other males follow her.

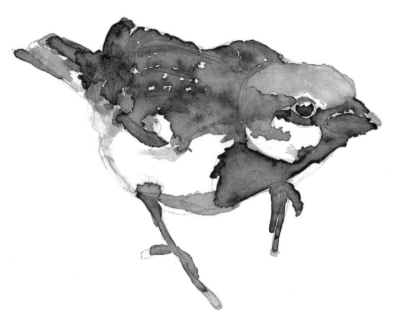

Dead Sea sparrow (*Passer moabiticus*)

There was a radio in every room of our house. My mother put the music on whenever she entered a room, even early in the morning when she went into the bathroom and then into the dressing room, which until recently had been Sabine's room and where now she ironed the washing for a dentist's surgery. Music blared through the whole house. It didn't bother me, because it meant that I didn't need to worry about my mother. The bathroom smelled of her sweet perfume. A brush, mascara, tweezers, lipstick and creams lay on the glazed shelf below the mirror.

The evening before my father's funeral my mother stood in the bathroom at the washbasin and cut off her hair. She injured her scalp as she did it, and the cuts bled heavily. My mother examined her face in the mirror, wept and then vomited over the strands of her hair in the basin and on the floor. Sabine screamed at her that she should stop, that it was all her fault after all. Sabine came home only briefly for the funeral and then vanished again.

Thursday 8 May 2003

I wake up very early, shuffle to the washrooms. The camp is quiet, like our village back home when I used to get up early in the morning in the school holidays to deliver the papers with Mrs Haas. She was small and fat and exceptionally bow-legged. When she laughed crow's feet formed around her eyes. For decades Mrs Haas distributed the local newspapers in our village. I pulled the cart with the bundles of newspapers. Mrs Haas told me about the barn by the river, which was still there, where Ambrosius's cottage had once been. After the paper round I had breakfast at home with Father and Sabine. My mother had already been gone six months by then. She called from time to time, when her new boyfriend was not at home. My father had begun training for the high jump again, something that had been a passion of his before but which he had given up after I was born.

As I think of all this, I am standing in the washing block under the shower, watching how the water runs down over my chest and stomach. I'm too skinny, I think, I have too little muscle for my height. Perhaps that's why I've never had much success with women. I'm not as clever as the others – Jan, Sergei, Julian. Maybe it's because I'm stupid that I just look at the same things for so long, over and over again, until they disappear inside me, perhaps that's why I like bird-watching so much. I've always thought that nobody liked me. I'm a beanpole, just like my father, supple and fit only for the high jump, if anything. But I've always refused in front of the bar, like a stubborn donkey, not believing, as my father did, that by performing an elegant high jump a man can, in a sense, fly.

After I've showered and put on my uniform I go to the canteen. On the way there I see a Russian tortoise in the entrance to its burrow. It is olive green and about as big as my palm. Its forelegs have four toes with strong claws, which it uses to bury itself in the loamy soil as soon as it gets hot in early June and the vegetation has withered. It stays there without feeding until the autumn. Now in the spring it is filling up on the sprouting vegetation and seeking mates to breed. In the autumn it will emerge again from its loam burrow for a short time, take in sustenance and then disappear into the earth for the whole winter.

I bump into the intelligence officer, as I do almost every morning. While we are standing next to each other at the food counter I can read his name badge: Oliver Levier. He always sits alone at the breakfast table, leafing through documents, making annotations in pencil, from time to time scratching his neck with his index finger, an uncommonly long finger, which he bends and uses like a hook. He drinks a cup of coffee at the same time and bolts down his breakfast carelessly. Sergei told me that Levier's unit is responsible for drone sorties, working with the Americans. Most of them are pilots or computer scientists, tasked with programming flight paths or steering drones.

The manuscript pages had dried out; the writing had run in places. Helena sat herself down on the floor and gazed at the drawings of the birds. She was astonished there were so many birds of such beauty in Afghanistan. On the news they showed only shattered cities, ruins, dusty streets where honking, ramshackle cars drove beside overstuffed buses, loud music coming from radios mingled with the surging and subsiding call of the muezzin. Paul wrote of veiled women whose coloured clothes fluttered in the wind, of children playing by the side of the street, men in baggy trousers and gold-embroidered caps. She smelled oriental spices, musty cow stalls, the sweat of fear; she listened to the cries of the wounded, she saw mangled bodies lying in the road and soldiers patrolling through villages, weapons at the ready. Paul told of how he had accompanied a reconstruction squad on a visit to a village in which the Taliban had destroyed a school for girls. Their mission was to talk to the mayor. They dismounted from their armoured personnel carrier at the edge of the village and marched along ditches. Paul was carrying his heavy combat medic's rucksack and an assault rifle, like the infantrymen. Two attack vehicles followed behind them. Everything was peaceful: children were fetching water in a can, old people were sat in front of their houses. The mayor was at his prayers in the mosque, forcing them to wait for two hours until finally the platoon commander of their squad could have a conversation with him. As usual, Paul described the birds he was able to see during their mission. After the meeting, the mayor disappeared behind the mud wall of his farm. On the way back to their transport they were shot at without warning; one of Paul's comrades was seriously wounded. Paul crawled over to him and treated him at the risk of his own life.

She read a few lines before laying the sheet back down and picking another page. Here Paul described the elaborate ornamentation on the townhouses, poppy fields and oases, a grand bazaar swarming with people, a palace decorated in blue mosaic, white doves in a park suddenly taking to the air like a cloud heavy with snow, the turquoise lake near the camp again. What was it about this lake, she wondered, that made Paul write about it over and over? She didn't leave the room until evening, shortly before Ignatz came home from work. She locked the door, because she was afraid Ignatz might walk into the room and a gust of wind would send the pages spinning.

Friday 9 May 2003

Friday is Afghanistan's Sunday, my duties don't start until 1300 hours. In the early morning I am sitting by the Hesco wall and looking in the direction of the helicopter pad when a small ringed plover flies away over me, calling. Moments later several European bee-eaters (*Merops apiaster*) announce their presence with warbles and trills. Bee-eaters are colourful harlequins, turning somersaults in the air to snap up bees and other insects. Afterwards they perch on the barbed wire and feed each other. It's a miracle that not a single bird has yet injured itself on the knife-sharp barbs. After a little while, an unfamiliar, fast-approaching call from another bird catches my attention. Through my binoculars I can see wings like a tern's, the curving flight and white underside suggest some kind of pratincole. It might even be a small pratincole. I would have had to examine a narrow white strip on the rear edge of the wings to tell the species apart. As I don't know for sure, I record the specimen as a pratincole on my bird-watching list. The Russian tortoises get a mention as well. Actually they distract me from the birds, and for some time I watch their leisurely activities. Perhaps they're the same ones as yesterday morning.

Theresa was complaining about how much her finger joints were hurting last time she called. Her hands are covered in cracks and fissures. In the evening she rubs glycerine ointment into her hands and the next day, as soon as she mucks out the stables, they tear open again. The truth is they are cheap servants, required to work from morning to night before falling bone-weary into bed. I ask her if she's heard anything from Jan. She wants to visit him, as soon as she has the free time. Theresa talks about the horses with pretty names – Bahadur, Espinosa, Smilla. About the young vet who comes to the farm almost every day. The valuable horses belong to wealthy people from the city, who have stabled their animals at the farm and pay a lot of money for their care. Sometimes they drop in, go out riding for a few hours, return and then give up their horses again.

European bee-eater (*Merops apiaster*)

Saturday 10 May 2003

In the south there have been skirmishes between the government forces and Taliban fighters. In the early morning we drive out of the camp in a heavily guarded convoy. We have to supply a hospital with medicines and offer medical assistance. They have no drugs, no dressings, no sterilisers, no anaesthetic machines. The rear of our transporter is stuffed with oxygen cylinders, sleeping bags, stretchers for patients, water canisters and food supplies. We perch wedged in amongst it all. I glance out through an opened shooting slit. The sun rises, and soon the sky is drenched in a deep blue. The sides of the road are lined with shacks made of wooden planks and rusty corrugated iron. In between, shirtless boys wearing baggy trousers caked in filth play next to burned-out Soviet tanks and abandoned weapons. After two hours, we arrive at the hospital, a grey building. In the courtyard within, patients are cooking their meals over an open fire. They are sitting under a tamarisk tree, its pink-coloured needles gleam in the sun and cast trembling points of light and shade on to the dusty ground. We park our transport in the courtyard, disembark, walk through shadowy corridors that stink of disinfectant and food. The facilities compare to those of a German hospital in the fifties. Women shrouded in burkas sit on benches with their children.

A girl, around ten years old, is lying on the treatment table. Crates of medicine are being carried in while I remove her dirty dressing. The soldiers open them noisily, placing what we've brought into metal cabinets. I can hear voices from the courtyard. I want to do a neat job, and I'm sweating from every pore. The girl's mother stands next to us, I can see only her eyes and hands. The child glances at the spinning blades of the ceiling fan. I laugh, I talk to her, she cannot understand me. She has deep burns on her abdomen, chest and underarms, affecting the entire skin layer and the bones that lie beneath. My fingers shake as I cut away the absorbent dressing, sticky with blood and pus. I'm trying to loosen the gauze as carefully as I can. The girl must be in extreme pain, but there's not a sound from her, she only presses her lips together, tears running down her cheeks, looks mutely to her mother. At some point this little girl will start to wear a burka too and from then on only her black eyes will be seen. The captain comes out of the second treatment room and glances at her wounds. A thin parchment-like skin has formed over part of them. 'That's actually healing better than I expected,' he declares. I spray antiseptic on to the wound and carefully apply a new dressing.

Monday 12 May 2003

Julian wants to become an officer. Accordingly, his kit must always be perfect, he reads books on military tactics and strategy for senior officers, goes to the gym every day and jogs through the camp wearing his rucksack, packed with his dumb-bells. After his time here, Julian wants to take the selection test and hopes that after that he can attend the German Armed Forces University. I don't know what I'll do after this. I don't even know if I want to go home. Perhaps I'll die here. I often think that, when I'm lying in my bed at night and can't get to sleep. As soon as our patrol or mission stops at the roadside, I'm watching the birds. I lean back against the tyres of our transporter and scan the area with my binoculars.

Carefree and elated, I ride my faithful mule onwards, over paths of hard-trodden earth, between spacious hillsides embroidered with flowers and the airy, soft-as-silk limpid mountain skies, it seems to me indeed as if there were here a multiplicity of skies, each one outdoing the others in its beauty. As my astonished gaze roams over it, this fair land appears to me like a new world, of paradisiacal valleys, one cannot imagine any more splendid, fertile plains running upwards to the snow-gleaming mountain ranges of the Hindu Kush, which by night look as if giants had hung up their cloaks in the sky. All this causes in me the greatest delight, and I do not know how to thank Almighty God enough for it. This journey has hitherto exceeded all my expectations in the most blissful way. I am as of now in the fruitful, myth-enshrouded valleys of Bamiyan. I stand marvelling in front of statues of Buddha perhaps a thousand feet in height carved from red sandstone, which stand nobly on this very site in alcoves of rock. According to the travelogue of Xuanzang, these statues were once covered in gold and decorated with jewels. Around these solemn gods are passageways and galleries hewn from the rock, prayer halls and cave homes. Some are richly furnished with wall paintings; others are simple and bare, as befits a room for meditation. A monastery of rock, where I stop to rest and stay a month in meditation, before I continue my pilgrimage, following ancient trade routes, which once made this land prosperous. I watch unknown birds, the loveliest creatures, their plumage blinding white over bluish, with jet-black wing tips, a bright-yellow beak and flecks of coral red, their lively eyes gleam, they are quite without shyness, but instead keep me company on my journey as if they were old acquaintances, settling themselves on my shoulders and twittering melodies in my ears, as trusted friends might offer secret whispers.

The Dingo has tinted glass for security. We drive along as if in a sealed capsule, as if we have been plunged into a deep, lightless sea. I think of Father – today would have been his birthday.

Since I've been living in the camp, I've noticed a strange peacefulness in myself, I've become much better at enduring, I feel as if time is simultaneously standing still and passing at furious speed, like in a spinning carousel, where I am living in the centre, in a state of suspense. I think about Jan and Theresa often. In my afternoon break I sit in front of the emergency medical centre. For the first time here I hear a hoopoe, a melodic sequence of muffled-sounding notes, as if it were playing a tune on a tiny reed pipe. No doubt it's sat on some lookout outside the camp, singing.

In the evening, when I have completed my duties, I lie wearily on my bed with my eyes closed. Julian talks incessantly about his shooting skills. We have known for a long time now that he is a good shot, he wears the silver marksmanship badge. Julian claims his eyesight is as sharp as a hawk's – a hawk that sees things we will never be able to make out.

My comrades throw darts at the dartboard on the wall over my bed. A dart speeds through the air, I hear it, how it pierces the disk of cork, how its shaft vibrates. Julian's dart hits the bull's eye every time. He says it's a good exercise in concentration, for shooting. I think I'm hearing sounds that are essentially impossible to hear.

Eurasian hoopoe (*Upupa epops*)

I lie in bed, keep my eyes closed and think of the evening when Theresa and I swam out into the middle of the maar. The day was hot and cooling off in the cold water refreshed us. Theresa is a good swimmer, I couldn't keep up with her. She glided along just under the surface of the water like a fish; as she swam her arms created glittering streaks. In the middle of the lake she took off her bathing cap, shook out her hair and waited for me next to a buoy. On the shore of the lake a small jetty stuck out through high reeds. Jan was sitting there, reading. He read whenever he had a few minutes of quiet and then told me about it later. Theresa kissed me. She wrapped her legs around my hips, said I needed to be absolutely calm or else we'd go under and drown. Small pieces of algae clung to her shoulders. Birds flew up from the reed beds by the shore. I saw their reflections on the water.

I haven't seen Theresa again since I left Kall, I haven't contacted her either. It amazes me, how a single moment in a life can change everything. Back then I only told Jan I was going into the army, but he couldn't understand me any more anyway. When I was driving around with him in the car, I was chauffeuring him all over, I spoke to him incessantly, complete bullshit too, like with a small child. These trips with Jan were the only thing I was doing back then. My mother was nagging me constantly, I drove until the fuel tank was empty, I was just hanging around, I wasn't making anything of my life. Perhaps she was afraid I might turn into Father. In the end, my call-up papers arrived. To me, they felt like a way out. During basic training and my training to become a combat medic, all I thought about was what I had to learn.

Saturday 17 May 2003

Bombardment. I hear missiles whistling, their muffled impact in the fields, then the pattering rain on our roof, my friends' breathing, Sergei moaning softly in his sleep.

By now the last of the migratory birds have returned from their winter habitats. I watch a European roller (*Coracias garrulus*) on the security wire on the far side of the prohibited area. What a gorgeous bird! Once you've tuned in to its behaviour and appearance, you realise this place is swarming with rollers.

My comrades assume I'm using my binoculars to keep watch for potential dangers. The sunlight and glimmering air in this country transform the plumage of the birds into silhouettes of some unreal thing.

European roller (*Coracias garrulus*)

Monday 19 May 2003

I spoke with Heinzmann, the staff sergeant, again and asked him for permission to visit the lake. It was a bad time to do it. He has placed a strict ban on leaving the camp, with good reason. Some of our soldiers were hit with small arms fire and RPGs in an ambush twelve kilometres from base, and a police headquarters has been attacked.

Maybe I'll never get to the lake. From the tower it seems to change in the sun, like a chameleon and its colours: in the evening it is a dark slate colour, then appears blue again, in the morning it is a shimmering green, like a forest lake. The shifts must be linked to the changing atmosphere, the interplay between clouds, light and reflection.

The guards on the watchtowers seem unobservant, in spite of the heightened state of alert. They spend most of the time playing cards or snoozing. They give the appearance of relying entirely on the electronic security system installed in the prohibited area between the Hesco walls and the perimeter fence. The system is supposed to trigger the alarm whenever a beam of light is broken. It's impossible to get through it and out of the camp. Getting to the shore of the lake is an obsession I have to give up.

Tuesday 20 May 2003

Back up on my tower, I'm watching black kites (*Milvus migrans*). They let a column of warm air carry them upwards, floating higher, seemingly without effort, in ever widening spirals, their wingspan outstretched, completely still save for scarcely perceptible flicks of some of their wing feathers. I have them perfectly in focus in my binoculars, I see how they answer each other with prolonged cries from their curved, wax-yellow beaks. I follow a young kite with cinnamon-coloured breast feathers and dark irises, notice how he corrects his trajectory. He is missing a couple of pinion feathers, but it doesn't seem to limit his soaring. I am looking so intently upwards that now there are only these gliding birds and their trails and pathways and roads in the sky, a world that for us will remain forever invisible. I corkscrew upwards with the soaring kites, high into the sky, shedding more and more weight until I lose sight of myself, until I can do what I have dreamed of ever since I was a child – fly. The kites are finally high up in the sky. With rapid shallow beats they build their velocity and dart away with their wings swept back.

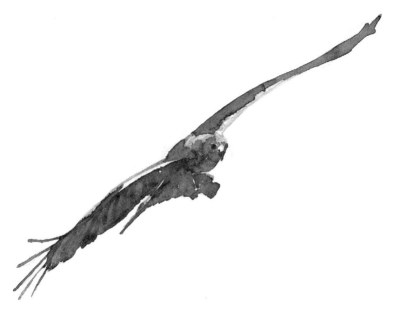

Black kite (*Milvus migrans*)

Wednesday 21 May 2003

I've decided I'm going to compile a book of birds' feathers. I buy black-and-white mounting card and glue from the camp shop. I've amassed a considerable number of feathers in the camp and on patrol, moult feathers from sparrowhawks and tits, a partridge feather and a flight feather, which I suspect originates from a shikra (*Accipiter badius*). Most ornithologists aren't particularly interested in feathers. Nature's wondrous filigree structures, both warm and cool, ornament and camouflage. Birds must have some kind of instinct for colour and beauty.

Nassim, who works in the shop, asked me what I was planning with the paper and glue. I told him. Nassim is tall, slim, around my age, speaks better German than my English. His eyes are full of nervous curiosity. We're so at home with each other, it's as if we've known each other our whole lives. Most of the civilian jobs in the camp are done by locals. They work in the canteen, the laundry, they lay the gravel paths and pave the squares, serve in the various shops and, if they speak German as well as Nassim, are employed as interpreters. Nassim has told me that he is studying business administration at Kabul University. He's working alongside his studies. As the eldest son, he is the head of the family and has to make a living for the others. The Taliban hanged his father, a pharmacist, from a crane in the market square. He hung there for several weeks, with a cardboard sign around his neck, saying that he was an unbeliever. Nassim had to walk across the square every morning on his way to school. One morning his father had disappeared, he had no idea where they had carted him off to. Nassim has two older sisters, a little brother and a blind grandfather. In the evening after his work in the camp, he goes home to his family, who live in a village nearby. Sometimes he goes for a walk out to the lake too. I tell him about my bird-watching. I speak, and as I do I see the lake in his curious eyes. He reminds me of Jan.

There is always someone speaking. We are incapable of lying silently in our beds, perhaps because we're so far from home, perhaps because the air conditioning mashes our odours into a pulp and in the darkness we don't know who we are any more, as if we have to talk constantly, to reassure ourselves that we are alive and not a mass of differing, fundamentally ego-less beings flying through the darkness in a vast flock.

I fall asleep, wake up again sweating and hearing Julian's voice. He's describing how he lived for a time in a children's home in Kall and why he never wants to go back there. Every morning on my way to school in Steinfeld our bus drove past the home where he must have been living back then. I mention Theresa, though I have no desire to talk about her. I must not tell them everything, I think, because if I tell them everything, it will disappear behind the words. Julian says he came across a girl called Theresa in Kall. He talks about the indoor pool, large fogged panes of glass, heated benches they used to lie on, of changing cubicles with holes in the partitions through which they used to spy on the other swimmers. I should describe my Theresa to him, but I don't want to get into it. He would only claim that he was talking about the same girl. I definitely never met Julian, not at the indoor pool, not at a football match, not at the funfair or in a disco, even though we're pretty much same age. Back then, when a group from the children's home came to the swimming pool, we made ourselves scarce, they were always looking to pick an argument for no reason, and we didn't want to get into a fight. Julian says he changed a lot during his time in Kall. I remember the groups of children walking from the station to the home. We didn't want to have anything to do with them. We were afraid of them, really.

Friday 23 May 2003

I've been watching the Dead Sea sparrows again. I've been listening to them every morning for a while now, they have their assembly point on our container and hold their morning roll-call there. They speak up one after the other, then chirrup in an excited tangle. It sounds like a related dialect to the language of the native sparrows, in the same way the language in the Eifel changes as you travel from one village to the next. I lie on my camp bed. I've closed my eyes. It's a troop of seven or eight sparrows. They are chatting animatedly with chirruping, rasping noises, sometimes they rant. They are pretty sad because they haven't got a female. I can understand them well, I can distinguish their voices, who has just begun to speak. I've given them names: one cheeps self-importantly like Hermann the captain of our medical team, another you hear only rarely, he makes me think of Nassim. The sparrows that haven't found a partner are all male and have their colony in an old Soviet tank and serve as helpers to the married pairs. When one of the married males dies, they will have the chance to take his place and win a female.

Father shook me awake in the early morning. We crept through the house so as not to disturb Mother and Sabine, rode our bikes through the cool, damp morning air into the Boletal down to the chalk quarry. I was eleven years old, it was the beginning of the summer holidays and I had my first year at grammar school behind me. We wanted to watch eagle owls, which nested in the abandoned quarry on the outskirts of the village. Father's bulging pannier was stuffed with our binoculars, bird-watching guides, a thermos of tea and sandwiches Father had prepared before he woke me.

We parked our bicycles at the perimeter fence of the quarry. Father lifted the lower strand of barbed wire so that I could crawl under easily. For a moment my face touched the still dew-soaked meadow, and I smelled chalky earth, velvet grass and moss. After I had wriggled my way through, as I still lay on the ground, I looked up into my father's smiling eyes. He took a run-up, and then leaped over the fence. He had been an avid high jumper in his youth, a regional champion, in fact. Jumping this fence was child's play to him. For my father, jumping hid within it the magic of flight. Though he had, unlike the birds, only the strength of his legs, nevertheless for a brief moment in this victory over an obstacle he seemed to feel weightless, he achieved the floating he had imagined, all bleak thoughts were gone. Father worked at the time in the cement works that had once owned the quarry. He often talked about his bird-watching and told fabulous stories of Ambrosius and the flying machine he built after he had returned to the village.

The Zeiss binoculars, 7×50, which my father used for birdwatching. When adjusting the eyepiece there is a tiny margin between absolute sharp focus and a blurred edge – a moment, comparable to the moment between reality and dream, remembering and forgetting.

Saturday 24 May 2003

A rocket lands in the middle of the camp in the night. Lying on my camp bed, I hear a whistling swelling and subsiding, then a muffled bang, like a firmly slammed door. I feel as if our world is a huge, contorted house of corridors, floors and doors. In some of the rooms, war reigns. At this moment, I don't know what my business is here.

Next morning I examine the impact site, a crater near the accommodation containers. Levier is standing at a distance, dazed. At the moment of the attack some of our soldiers were coming out of the bar. When they heard the whistling overhead they had the presence of mind to throw themselves to the ground and thus received only grazes. Shrapnel hit some of the containers and vehicles were damaged. There are rocket attacks like this several times a week, but most of the missiles fly right over the camp, landing in the prohibited area or the fields. They pose no threat to us.

We hear that five NATO soldiers have been killed in the east of the country: three of those died in an accident, one when a mine exploded and one was the victim of an insurgent attack. We don't know the nationality of the soldiers yet, a platoon from our unit was on patrol there at the time.

I have already been travelling for many months now. The days have quite run through my hands, too many thoughts and astonishments have made me forget the time. Travellers are always welcome in these lands, as I have been well able to observe; it suffices to say that one is on a journey and everywhere one is immediately hosted in the most friendly manner, with whatever little there may be. And yet it often happens, in this earthly paradise, that I spend the night under the open sky; at the end of the day I seek out a comfortable place to make camp on a hill covered in thick shrubs until at last I catch sight of a mysterious lake, glittering in the moonlight. Above it all, a star-strewn sky of inexplicable beauty. A gorgeously coloured Arcadia, no country the whole world round can rival it, not even Samarkand or Tabriz. One becomes aware of the vivid brown shades of earth and mountains, trails of smoke in the distance curling out of village huts, a cluster of poplars, every leaf sharply silhouetted in the shimmering, silken light. As I near a village I soon find myself ringed by a cheerful flock of children, who set about competing as to who amongst them might lead me to their parents' house, where I will be welcomed in the friendliest manner. Around me a carpet of small yellow quinces, which have been mashed under the hooves of my mule and unfurl a beguiling aroma on all sides. The footsteps of herds of camels are drawn in the dust like trefoils. All the splendour at the court of the Emperor Babur, a green sky, the colour of which will soon peel away; soon the songs of the birds will spread without end, those ringing sounds which I have followed this far, secret traces made of sound, a map made of dreams. A band of horsemen kicks up dust in the distance before finally disappearing over the horizon. In the emperor's gardens plants offer themselves to my eyes, trees, some blossoming, some already bearing fruit, vines and garden plants and other things that make for good eating, though most are quite foreign and unknown to me. Pomegranates, apricots, quinces, pears, peaches, plums, almonds, nuts and wine so intoxicating. In the Mughal's palace one could identify thirteen varieties of tulip, and I saw hundreds of birds I did not recognise

– each specimen more beautiful than the last in their golden cages – and listened in on a thousand sounds, so that I might note down with my quill the letters of their alphabet, which I am still lacking.

Sunday 25 May 2003

I dreamed of the lake last night, the surface of the water looked like cool molten glass. I perched on the shore behind the remains of the wall of a fisherman's house and watched the streaks and patterns of the waves, intertwined white lines. The water seems so shallow, as if you could wade through it across to the other shore.

Early in the morning I discover that a corporal from the mechanised infantry battalion has been found severely injured in the camp. In the field hospital they can only certify him dead. After their first investigations, they are proceeding on the basis of suicide. Strangely, the service pistol with which he is supposed to have inflicted the fatal head injury has not yet been found.

Monday 26 May 2003

In former times, farmers in the Hindu Kush dug in caves for lapis lazuli, a gemstone as blue as the sky here. Ambrosius wrote about white lizards, which lived in these caves and were about the size of an adult middle finger. They ran lightning fast along the walls, froze inert for hours at a time in one place, their bodies like breathing, milky light, the skin almost transparent, so that Ambrosius believed he could make out all their organs and their buried, degenerated wings. These lizards could sense everything in the darkness. At some point in the unending millennia of their lives, their eyes had become so adapted to their surroundings that they could no longer leave the caves. As the lizards no longer had eyelids, their pupils would be scorched by the sunlight outside. Then even they would no longer be able to sense the dark in the darkness.

Bomb attack in the city. The bombs exploded around midday and tore craters in the road. When we arrive two hours later, people are standing by the side of the road. I jump out of the Dingo, dash over to a bundle on the pavement, a man covered in dust. The explosion has torn the clothes from his body, blasted him into two halves, his bowels are scattered around him, one leg hangs over his shoulder. As I crouch down next to him, his chest rises and falls, then suddenly he is entirely without motion. I shrug on latex gloves, gather up the parts of his body, lay them on a blanket, and carry them to the ambulance.

Today, like pretty much every evening, Sergei telephones his wife. I walk outside and sit down in front of our container. There's still enough light to look out for birds. As I'm scanning the Hesco walls with my binoculars, five common mynah birds (*Acridotheres tristis*) are perching there. They're too far away for me to hear them, but from the movements of their beaks and the way they stretch their colourful heads forward and puff out the iridescent feathers of their necks, I can tell that they are chattering and singing. Mynahs are roughly the same size as our native German starlings but much more richly coloured. Their belly plumage is a dark brown, their head and wings are black, beak and feet a gleaming yellow and the hem of their tail feathers is white. Their eyes make you think of black pinheads, behind which lurks a fleck of naked, flashing yellow, which they, like some demonic Chinese wizard, can make appear. They can imitate human voices. I imagine that one of them speaks with Sergei's inflections, another yells like our sergeant and still others shriek like a group of romping children. The whole flock flies over our canteen to look for things to eat in the waste from the kitchen.

In the night I have to go out. I'm on standby. A helicopter is bringing in wounded who we will care for in the field hospital. An armoured personnel carrier, taking evasive action in a fire fight, has veered off the road and rolled over in a riverbed. One of the crew is severely injured, two less seriously. Shrapnel, gunshot wounds and injuries from the accident, so much blood, as much as in a Tarantino film. I assist in the operations. One of the soldiers has a bullet stuck next to his visual cortex and is flown back to Germany to a specialist hospital.

Common mynah (*Acridotheres tristis*)

My father trudges up the steep grassy slopes underneath the viaduct, stripping the panicles off the brome grass as he goes and putting the seeds in his trouser pocket. By daybreak, before the first cars drive along the motorway, he has arrived on the viaduct above, where we used to walk to watch the peregrine falcons. In my ever-recurring dream, my father stands on the carriageway, testing the wind direction with the seeds of grass, letting them trickle slowly out of his hand. Because the road isn't wide enough, he must begin his run parallel to the barrier. He has trained for a whole year and developed a new jumping technique.

Friday 30 May 2003

An Afghan fox is roaming about in the prohibited area between the Hesco wall and the perimeter fence. Its graceful movements remind me of a cat with a long, bushy tail. It forages and sniffs. Soon it is sitting motionless in front of a hole with its oversized bat ears pricked, waits, suddenly pounces in a single leap on a mouse and bites it dead. How did it get there? How did the electronic barriers not trigger an alarm? Perhaps it dug through under the fence, or its den has an exit into the prohibited area. In any case the electronic defences ought to have triggered an alarm. Perhaps they're faulty and no one in the watchtower has noticed yet. I don't know how often the technology is tested. If the fox can roam there, it must be possible for me to cross the area without the guards spotting me. I'm not going to suppress these thoughts any longer. I've decided to watch the guardposts, perhaps there is still somehow a possibility of leaving the camp unnoticed.

Shortly after midnight the drones are launching again, they take off from the back of a lorry, their engines ignite with a loud bang, they are flying to a target none of us knows.

In the morning I bump into Levier again. Apart from me, he's the only one hanging around in the mess hall so early. I make no attempt to talk to him, as he plainly wants to be left in peace. Levier has a broad, flat face with a small red nose and narrow, intelligent eyes. He sits, as always, at the head of the long table in the alcove behind the food counter. He bolts down his food like someone who has always lived alone. It's only here in the canteen, apparently, that he behaves so strangely. The moment he leaves he pulls himself together and acts normally. The office container for the Military Intelligence Unit sits in an area protected by Hesco walls and coils of wire, to which only staff officers have access. On the wall next to the entrance, they have fixed the tactical emblem of high command and the unit's motto: *scientia potestas est.*

Last night they flew hourly drone strikes into the restive region of North Waziristan. The area is a stronghold of both the Taliban and Al-Qaeda. Fourteen Islamists were killed in the strikes.

We live in this camp as if in a vast cage. I can hardly bear it any longer. While my comrades hang out at the gym or in the bar, I sit most of the time in our container, on my bed. I clean feathers, disinfect them, glue them to the mounting card. I add small descriptive cards to each page with details of where I found them. I have always liked touching feathers, holding them cautiously on the flat of my hand. They are hollow inside and so structured that the refraction and absorption of light creates shimmering colours, or else the bird ingests the colourings with its food and then stores them in its feathers. For most feathers, the colour contrasts are seen much more clearly against a dark card than a light one. The edges and gradients of the colour especially are much easier to make out, even with dark plumage.

The superb lyrebird (*Menura superba*) cannot stop singing in the middle of its courtship dance. The satin bowerbird (*Ptilonorhynchus violaceus*), found only in Australia, if deprived of the blue petals it needs to decorate its nest, will kill the first available blue bird to adorn its bower with the feathers.

In order to get off base again at last, I get permission from the captain to take part in firing practice outside the camp. Once we've passed through the main gate, we are driven for half an hour along surfaced roads, our transport staggers and jolts in potholes and ditches. It's impossible to focus my binoculars on the birds flying over the fields.

The shooting range is in a hollow. I spot a bird through the telescopic sight. It perches on the heaped-up wall of earth near to the target. A breeze ruffles the tips of its covert feathers, it has piercing yellow eyes. At first it looks around fearfully, but then it seems to have calmed itself and cleans its plumage, pulling on its feathers with its beak, tidying the vanes. The officer bawls me out, I should fire a shot at some point. With every shot I breathe in a mixture of gun smoke and dry, dusty clay. I fine-tune the scope until a series of shots in rapid succession hit the black. The officer is happy with my hit rate. Now I have time to explore the area. I climb out of the hollow and stand on a knoll thickly covered in steppe grass, walk further, sit down under the shade of a tree and take my helmet off. I can see the lake from here. Rippling waves form on the surface of the water, reproducing the traces of the wind. The shores of the lake are completely filled with flocks of coursers, moorhens, curlews and other species.

On my walk back I poke at the bleached-out skeleton of a laughing dove (*Streptopelia senegalensis*). The feathers on the shoulder blades have been matted together by dust and heavy rain. The dove was probably attacked by a peregrine falcon, which left its victim's wings unplucked. I take a beautiful tail feather, stick it in my helmet and walk back to the firing range.

Tuesday 10 June 2003

Today around midday the thermometer on the outside of our container burst. It did finally get cooler in the evening, but I'm still sweating. The others are going to the camp bar. It's pleasantly cool in the container, I've got used by now to the constant monotone hum of the air conditioning. I make entries in my diary, I try to sketch the ravens (*Corvus corax*) I spotted on the Hesco walls. They were perched together, cackling derisively, cleaning their coats of feathers as they gleamed in the shimmering heat, their beaks flashing like sharply honed blades.

I'm angry with the company commander, who has definitively forbidden me from going to the lake after the sergeant relayed my request up to him. If the electronic barrier is out of action, I only need to wait for the right moment, when the guards aren't paying attention. Sergei mentioned that he's made friends with the soldiers on guard duty, and if I absolutely want to go to the lake, he could talk to them, perhaps some opportunity might emerge.

Common raven (*Corvus corax*)

Saturday 14 June 2003

For several days the camp has been filled with excitement. A high-up general has announced he is visiting. Everything is being tidied and cleaned. I am fearful that someone will even clean the old Russian tank and destroy the clutches of the Dead Sea sparrows in the process. Luckily two containers have been installed that block the view of the scrapyard and the tank.

Up in the sky I spot a male skylark (*Alauda arvensis*). He whistles and quavers, climbing ever higher as he does so, until it's almost impossible to make him out, then he glides back to earth, wings outstretched and tail fanned out, landing behind the Hesco wall.

We have formed up in rows, we have to hold out in the vicious heat. Finally the helicopter appears in the distance. The rotor blades spin the dust into the air, making it harder to land, we disappear in the dust, we mustn't budge. The skids touch down. The loading ramp opens, three escorting officers, stooped under the spinning rotor blades, run on to the rostrum, the general strides past us, a short little man in dust-covered glasses greets us and climbs up on to the podium built especially for him, cleans his glasses with a cloth handed to him by the adjutant and then addresses the crowd. The lark has soared upwards again and is singing high above the prohibited area.

Monday 16 June 2003

In the evening I talk to my mother on the phone. She passes on greetings from Theresa. She says that Theresa visited Jan in Kall and afterwards waited for the train with Mother in the café. A man dropped by, had a coffee with Theresa, then she drove off with him in his practice van. I lie on my bed, my hands interlocked behind my head, I glance at the starry sky through the small window, I taste dust and, though I am tired, I cannot get to sleep, too many thoughts are circling in my head.

Tuesday 17 June 2003

The night is unbearably hot. I sit on my bed, writing a letter to Jan, I tell him my plan to walk to the lake, I promise I'll report back to him what birds I see on its shore, though I know he has never really been interested in birds. The moment my eyelids are shut, Julian and Sergei arrive back from the bar. Later, when the two of them have dozed off, I get dressed in the dark and go for a walk through our camp-village. The only light still burning is coming from the chapel, a sort of hut built of brick, hardly bigger than a phone booth, with a silver cross on its gable and a picture of Christ inside. I sit down on the steps in front of the entrance and watch the eyed hawk-moths (*Smerinthus ocellata*) and other moths I don't recognise fluttering around the light. Later I climb up on to my viewing platform. The wind blows cooler up there. The mirror lake reflecting in the moonlight looks much nearer than it really is. I lean with my back against the parapet, listen to the trilling of a marsh warbler and imagine that it learns many other bird languages on its wanderings, every language of every land it passes through on its migration – a small, polyglot maestro of song. It draws an acoustic map of its itinerary, a journal of tones. No doubt it is hatching its eggs in the reeds on the shores of the lake, but for now it will sit on a bush somewhere and sing.

Our lives are not like the lives of birds, we can never be so certain as they can. Our language decays, we never hit the right melody, because our thoughts and our habits change too quickly.

White bats and pipistrelles flap around the tower, they come so near me I could catch them with my bare hands. The closer dawn comes, the more the number of singers grows, it's as if they want to outdo each other. The chirruping of a redstart (*Phoenicurus phoenicurus*) accompanies the rising sun, the mountain peaks of the Hindu Kush gleam in the distance, gulls and coursers circle over the lake. I imagine there are many species of bird there as yet unseen. The crown of barbed wire makes it more or less impossible to climb over the perimeter fence, which surrounds the prohibited area. I will have to dig a hole under the fence, then crawl for sixty metres, hoping the guards don't spot me, before finally, on the far side of the dyke, running to the lake, bent over, hidden by a ditch. I can let myself down the Hesco wall into the prohibited area with a rope, I can hide the cord in the cracks between the ashlars. I am devising new plans all the time. Above all, I need to pay attention to the guards, how they behave, I should be watching them every day to learn their habits. Sergei promised me he would talk to his friends. He's going to let me know when they're on duty in the guard tower. A lot of things would be easier if they would simply look the other way.

Redstart (*Phoenicurus phoenicurus*)

We parked in front of Jan's parents' house. Theresa was still crying. She was wearing a crocheted cap, her curly hair spiralling out from underneath it. A cloth bag with poppies embroidered on it lay on her lap. Single threads had come loose from their blooms where she had picked at them. Theresa was angry and hurt. I had only just told her that I'd had my call-up papers and would be going away. She refused to get out of the car, so I got out by myself, walked around the vehicle and opened the boot to check on the marten; by this time it had been in there the whole afternoon and was making a racket in its cage. When it saw me, its restless eyes flashed fearfully at me. I'd promised Mother that I would finally abandon it somewhere. I closed the boot carefully and walked through Jan's parents' front garden. It was unusually mild for the end of October. Mosquitoes were dancing under the trees. Odette opened the door, dried her hands on her smock. 'Come in,' she said. 'Georg is just helping Jan get dressed.' Since Jan's accident, Odette didn't have the zest for life she used to have and Georg hardly spoke. He worked at Raiffeisen Bank in a nearby town, but he didn't answer the telephone any more. His only task was to check over accounts, and I suspected he wasn't even doing that now. A black 1950s telephone stood on a bureau, one of those with a rotary dial and a heavy handset on a cradle; somehow it suited this house of quarried stone which Georg had been renovating for years. A steep staircase ran up to the first floor, where Jan's room was. In the old days, when I came to visit Jan, I'd have run up to see him straight away. From there we'd have scrambled out on to the garage roof, where we would sit for hours at a time, listening to music and looking out over the river. Jan was so helpless now, I couldn't bear it. I preferred to wait in the kitchen with Odette until Georg came down with Jan. She asked me about Theresa. I told her about Theresa's plan to begin training as a professional groom and about my call-up papers. 'I'd never have thought you'd go into the army,' said Odette. She was cutting onions and mushrooms on the sideboard. Last autumn I had collected mushrooms with Jan: chanterelles, porcini and parasols. In the evening we had prepared the mushrooms with Odette and Georg, eaten them together in the dining room, drunk wine and played the fool. Odette asked me what my plan was for Jan today. 'We'll just go for a little drive around the area. He likes that,' I said. I wanted to find a suitable spot to release the marten, but of course I didn't say anything about that. 'Sometimes my boy doesn't recognise me any more,' said Odette. I think maybe she wanted to say something further, but just then Georg came down the stairs with Jan. Jan was clutching the banister with both hands, he was walking sideways, placing one foot carefully in front of another, like a child who has only just learned to walk. Georg was holding him. 'We're going to have a stair-lift installed,' remarked Georg. He was wearing tracksuit bottoms, bits of food were stuck to his pullover. In the old days Georg always wore a suit and a white shirt, he was dressed like that even in his free time, as if he might go to work at the bank at any moment. Odette wiped the spittle from Jan's mouth with her handkerchief, helped him into his lumberjack's coat and placed a baseball cap on his head. She embraced him and suddenly began to cry. As we were saying goodbye she said she ought to say hello to Theresa. But Theresa wasn't sitting in the car any more. She'd written on a scrap of paper that it was over, she couldn't take my lies any longer. In the boot the marten hissed. I drove off. Jan leaned against the passenger window and stared at the flapping flags of the supermarket, where my mother had gone back to work in the café after Father had died. Sacks of rock salt and snow tyres on palettes sat in front of the café. The marten had quietened down again. We drove along country roads, past the sewage plant to the cement works where my father used to work. Jan slobbered, threads of spit dropped on to his jumper. As we curved through the landscape, I protested my innocence over and over. 'It was an accident.' Jan nodded, but then he nodded at everything anyone said to him. I pulled up in a layby, wiped his mouth, went to the boot and had a look at the marten. It was bleeding, perhaps it had injured itself on the bars of the cage or bitten itself. It smelled terrible. I slammed the boot shut and drove on through the Dalbenden valley. Jan was enjoying looking at the outdoors. His scrawny fingers plucked at the legs of his trousers, he began to hum. 'Would you like it if we paid the Medusa a visit?' I asked. In the old days we spent a lot of time with the Medusa. She watched over an old Roman well, water that had flowed in a stone channel through the Eifel as far as Cologne. I parked at the edge of the wood, helped Jan out of the car and got the marten's cage out of the boot. We walked along the river for a bit. Jan's walk was a waddle, he stopped often, the marten in the cage didn't interest him. Odette had said that Jan had to have another operation. Perhaps then he would be able to walk properly again. Perhaps at some point things would be again as they once had been. We left the path, crossed a meadow and continued our walk along a railway embankment next to the rails. The Medusa head loomed out of the wall around the well. Jan walked closer, he touched the snake tresses, as he used to, back when he was still healthy. I gathered wood for a campfire. As the fire burned, I sat down next to Jan and opened the hatch of the marten's cage. The animal darted out and vanished into the dusk.

Wednesday 18 June 2003

The Persian name for my lake, دریاچه آرام (*deryāche ārām*), means 'Silent Lake'. Nassim says that as a young boy he used to trap birds there with his grandfather and sell them at the market in Kabul. He talks about a fantastical bird market, almost everyone here keeps one of these little animals in their house. His compatriots loved birds, but that certainly didn't stop them eating them as well. The big species especially have been shot and eaten since the war started. Even the children have guns now, he says. The Persian name for the magpie is پرستو (*perestu*).

There are not five distinct species. Perhaps they died out a long time ago, or perhaps it was all a figment of Ambrosius's imagination.

I tell Nassim that I intend to climb over the Hesco walls and run to the lake. I finally have a plan. I know the moment when I will take the risk. Perhaps I'll meet up with Nassim there. He's at the lake sometimes, I can see him from my tower. Most of the time he's perched on the old wall of a fisherman's hut, which was blown to pieces by the Russians and which is supposed to have belonged to his uncle.

Thursday 19 June 2003

We travel eastwards on a mission. On the far side of the Kabul Gorge, Tang-e Gharu, I spotted several drongos and song thrushes, near Jalalabad Indian pheasant-tailed jacanas and sunbirds. Nassim, as our interpreter, sits with our convoy's platoon commander. We are on the road for three days altogether. I sit with my comrades at the back of the transporter, our rucksacks between our legs, we have so little room we can barely move. You can only see anything in our short breaks. The landscape becomes greener and greener, and I feel myself remembering the volcanic Eifel.

On the last day of our return journey a sandstorm catches us by surprise. In an instant all animals have vanished, an oppressive silence descends, the sky turns purple and visibility is reduced to a few metres, then terrifying quantities of sand roll towards us. Filled with sand and dust, the area around us soon resembles a vast hourglass. The storm ends as abruptly as it began. Around midday we finally make it back to camp and unload the vehicle in the blistering heat. We disinfect the medical equipment thoroughly, disassemble, clean and then reassemble our weapons. I fall asleep midway through the work. Later that evening I carry my sweat-soaked uniform to the collection point. An Afghan firm collects our laundry.

I sleep all day Sunday until Sergei wakes me in the evening. He says he's spoken to his friends, tells me the rota for the guards. There are Afghan soldiers as well, however, who are likely to shoot at anything that moves. So I had better be especially wary of the Afghans. When Julian comes into our container, we change the subject, chat about trivial things. He mustn't find out, he'd want to dissuade me from doing it, or report me. I fall back to sleep and dream of the lake.

Drongo (*Dicrurus macrocercus*)

Early in the morning, on my way to the canteen, I discover some young Dead Sea sparrows, hatched this spring, on the roof of a container. They're easy to recognise from the swollen yellow corners of their mouths at the base of the beak. Sparrows can fly as soon as they leave the nest. Whereas we have to learn everything first, even the basics.

In the canteen Levier is standing at the serving counter, drawing coffee out of the machine, his hands are trembling, he places the cup down on his tray and shoves it along to the glass cabinet with the sandwiches. His face is paler than usual, he has forgotten to tie his shoelaces. On the way to the table he trips, the cup of coffee, his documents, the plate with the sandwich, all fall to the floor. For a time he stands there, his arms suspended in front of him, and stares at this mishap, shaking his head as if he cannot grasp what has happened. Only when the kitchen boy comes over, picks everything up and wipes down the damp, smeared documents, does he return to consciousness, yanks the papers from the young man's hand, gets himself a new coffee and goes wordlessly to his place at the table.

Tuesday 24 June 2003

Yesterday I was in the camp library again. There's no air conditioning, so no one stays in the container long. A desk stands in front of the window with a laptop on it, which has a slow internet connection, making it essentially unusable. The sticky, hot air smells of books from the collections of broken-up libraries back home. There is no supervision. If you want to borrow a volume, you just take it. I flick through Goethe's *Poetry and Truth*, I read: *All contentment in life is founded on the regular return of external things. The cycle of day and night, the seasons, the blossoms and fruits, and whatever else presents itself to us from epoch to epoch, so that we can and should enjoy it, these are the mainsprings of earthly life. The more open we are to these pleasures, so much the happier we will feel; but if the variety of these phenomena rolls up and down before us without our having a part in it, if, in the face of such gracious offerings, we are unmoved, then enters the greatest evil, the heaviest sickness: man looks upon life as a loathsome burden.*

I am afraid.

A little further on, on the next page, it says under the heading 'Weariness of Life' (*Radix malorum est*): *Nothing prompts this weariness more than the return of love.*

We fly by helicopter to the mountain slopes of the Hindu Kush. Looking at this vast mountain chain, I remember that, according to Ambrosius, there is supposed to be a secret entrance into the earth somewhere there. A cave, which leads into the innards of a central sphere, a sphere itself encircled by concentric hollow spheres. The earth is located, according to this, in a vast grotto, with a sky, stars, sun and unknown long-extinct species of bird.

Narrow river valleys, oases and flower gardens, we fly towards the mountain slopes, which from a distance appear barren but up close reveal fertile arable plains and fields of sunflowers and poppies. Fields of plants I do not recognise, which will be harvested by farmers with sickles and carried to the village in great bundles on donkeys. On the flight back, as we near the lake, flocks of birds ascend.

I recognise some red-rumped swallows and then, high up in the sky, at first discernible only as dots, three griffon vultures, flying north towards the Salang Pass.

Thursday 3 July 2003

After work, a meeting about tomorrow's mission. We will be travelling for a week, as far as the border with Pakistan. It's very dangerous down there. A British patrol was attacked there just recently, insurgents destroyed their vehicles with booby traps and mines. I'm not going to have any time to look at birds or make notes on this mission.

On my way from the medical container to the canteen I hear yellowhammers calling in the dusk. To me it sounds like a song of farewell. I stand there listening to their singing, a series of short introductory tones followed by an extended concluding section, constantly varying. The yellowhammers (*Emberiza citrinella*) are perched in a bush next to the laundry. I can actually work out the approximate age of each singer from the small pauses between their melodic piping. Perhaps they are speaking to each other in a language both comprehensive and enduring.

In the night I am sweating again, I cannot sleep, the whirring noise of the air conditioning drives me close to madness. I would love to disconnect it, but my comrades would kill me if I did.

Yellowhammer (*Emberiza citrinella*)

Tuesday 15 July 2003

Back from the mission, the air is hot and sluggish. Except for an isolated summer storm, nothing has changed for two days. Our time here is filled with waiting, with the endlessly repeating work at the camp field hospital and the sick bay and, occasionally, a mission. We wait to report for duty every morning, we wait for news from home. (I've heard nothing from Theresa for a long time now.) I've got into the habit of going to the library. No one except me ever goes there anyway, so I lower the blind, leaving only a narrow gap, take off my uniform and perch in my underwear on the armchair at the desk. A single strip of light, particles of dust dancing within it, falls on the tabletop and the bookshelf behind me. In my imagination the books are dissolving in the intense heat, turning into flickering dust, which clings to my skin and enters my lungs. I drink water, I sweat, I read.

Over and over I ask myself what led me to this country, this war. This war which seems to me now like some lurking beast with a thousand grotesque faces.

When I get back from the library to our container Sergei is sitting on the bed on the phone to his wife. Usually by now he's already in the bar with his friends. I sense that something isn't right. To avoid disturbing him, I go back outside and sit myself down in front of our container.

Saturday 19 July 2003

I can't sleep again. I wander restlessly around the camp. I have just for the first time in my dreams heard the voices of birds, but when I woke I could no longer remember the tune, which had seemed to me more like an unknown language. It is still dark, cicadas (*Auchenorrhyncha*) chirrup, moths flutter in the dim light of a lamp. I hunker down on a crate somewhere. Two more weeks, then the guard units will change over – finally I can try to make it to the lake.

As dawn breaks I spot a fox in the prohibited area, prowling around, sniffing, evidently it considers the zone to be its hunting ground. Central command hasn't noticed that the electronic barriers are faulty and the guards seem not to care. They spend their shifts drinking and playing cards.

I hear the drones starting up again. What targets have Levier and his team programmed into them? When I see him each morning in the canteen, I have the urge to sit down next to him, chat with him. But he is too immersed in his own world, I'll get nothing from him. As he studies his papers, he scratches his neck constantly with his long fingers, always the same spot. Sometimes it bleeds, and he wears a scarf to hide the wound.

Thursday 24 July 2003

The air conditioning has broken. We have hordes of tiny, vile sandflies in our container. Julian is standing naked on his bed, flailing around with a hand towel – there are thousands of biting flies, which carry leishmaniasis, the more we kill, the more take their place. They settle themselves on every part of the body, in the corner of your eye, in your ears and nostrils, biting and then sucking out our blood to pass on the protein to their eggs. We make jokes, we say that the flies out here are as crazy about Julian's body as the women back home. He is covered in tiny inflamed spots. The insects are plaguing all of us, but Julian has a particularly bad reaction to the bites, his face, neck and eyes have swollen up. Raging, he hits every fly with his hand towel, on the wall, on the ceiling, on the furniture. Soon there are flecks of blood everywhere. We engage the enemy together, now all of us are hitting in all directions with our towels, leaping around the container with music blaring, screaming 'Attack!', laughing at ourselves and sweating like we're in a sauna. Suddenly Julian lurches and falls to the ground, we didn't know that he has an allergy to fly bites. When he comes round I want to take him to the medical tent, but he won't go with me, he's afraid it could have negative consequences for his assessment, that they will send him home. When we think we've killed all the flies, we turn out the light and try to sleep. After a short time in the dark we hear the buzzing again.

The principality of Kabul is assigned to the fourth climate zone and is situated at the centre of the inhabited world, whose cloak is the endless firmament. The population congregate in wondrous gardens, stroll about, around noon ensconce themselves in the acacia groves for their luncheon and in the afternoon hours attend equestrian games or fly colourful kites for love and luck. The caravans, which come from Kashgar, Fergana, Turkestan, Samarkand or Bukhara, know to stop over in the city and peddle their wares in the markets, the finest silk cloths and crystalline salts from the mountains. Merchants continue from Kabul to China and Asia Minor. In the cities the curious eyes of travellers are met by the colourfully painted doors of splendid houses; in the shadows of a hallway the amber-coloured eyes of a lovely woman, the laughing faces of her children. Minarets too, the swelling calls of the muezzin, fumes from samovars and delicious tea are advertised in a multiplicity of tongues – Arabic, Persian, Turkish, Mongolian, Hindi, Pashto – blending with the carols of the birds. On the roofs the white tangle of clattering and hissing storks. Carpet tents, kiosks selling every kind of precious object fringe the bazaars, camels whose foreheads are festooned with many-coloured pearls against the evil eye, mule drivers load their animals with contraband in the early morning, set off to cross the Hindu Kush on twisting, secret trails. Next spring I will join up with them and return to my home. In the bazaar I catch sight of birdcages elaborately wrought out of silver wire; tradition tells us that the Mughal emperors had sumptuous aviaries built in their palace gardens.

I smoke hashish with gorgeous dark-skinned women, mistresses of the arts of love.

Sunday 27 July 2003

I hear the voices of birds more and more often in my dreams. It feels like a melody torn apart. Often in the middle of the day during a mission, I want to go to sleep and hear this melody, it seems to transform everything.

From the tower I watch swifts, swallows and bulbuls. The bulbuls are the size of thrushes, a little slimmer, a small tuft sprouts on their heads and their cheeks are coloured red. Most of the time they perch in the crown of barbed wire on the fence and allow themselves to be thoroughly observed, as if they know that I revere them. When they fly, they remind me of woodpeckers, beating their wings three times and then gliding an undulating course through the air. Today the bulbuls let me watch them for almost half an hour, then fly away in the direction of the lake. The evening sun glitters on the water.

Bulbul (*Pycnonotus jocosus*)

Wednesday 30 July 2003

In the evening, after spending some time in the library, I go for a walk through the camp. I have stuck my binoculars and bird book in my pocket, hoping I can make some observations, so long as there's light. I have to figure out how the guards operate and check whether the fox is still in the prohibited area. A convoy stands in front of the entry gates, they've just come back from patrol. The guards check the underside of the vehicles with a mirror before they'll allow them to pass. I sit down, leaning against the Hesco wall, and look over at my comrades. Nassim exits the camp and rides off on his bicycle down the dusty country road in the direction of the village.

The Taliban have stayed quiet these last weeks. No one is expecting an attack on the camp – still less that someone might have the idea to get out of the camp over the Hesco wall. It's too crazy a move – and that's my chance. I'm counting the days now until finally everything will be ready. Red-tailed bumblebees, which have built their nests between the walls, land on flowers that look like our own coltsfoot. The Russian tortoises have already disappeared into their burrows. It's become too hot for them.

A gaudy carrot-tailed gecko crawls around on my trousers fearlessly. I am able to observe it carefully. Three more days, and the guard changes. I hope that the electronic barrier isn't repaired before then, though I know that according to regulations they're supposed to be tested regularly. I have already made all my preparations for my excursion.

Saturday 2 August 2003

At last, today is the day. After night duty in the sick bay, I meander through the containers, tents and radio masts. Apart from a couple of early risers, no one else is about. The last few nights I've not slept for excitement. I go to the spot where the Hesco wall is only three and a half metres high. I look around, then climb up the steel mesh of the wall – from the camp out there's no problem, but from the outside on my way back I'll need a rope to make it up the wall. I stand for the first time in the prohibited area. It's thirty metres to the perimeter fence, which is topped with a tangle of barbed wire no one could climb over. I run, throw myself to the ground in front of the fence and dig a hole with my folding shovel in the soft sandy ground until finally I am able to crawl through into the open field beyond. I crawl slowly forwards with the feeling that the guards are looking in my direction. I crouch motionless in a ditch, no shade, the air is so hot that I am sweating even though I am rooted to the spot. I have the feeling I am slowly desiccating, I am crumbling to dust. Carefully I drink a swig from the small water bottle I'm carrying in the leg pocket of my trousers. Then I faint. When I come round, it's dark. I have to hurry to be back before the changing of the guard.

On my way back I see nightjars (*Caprimulgus aegyptius*). In the darkness I can only identify them by the white flashes on their wingtips and the ends of their tails, I hear their monotonous churring as they whirr through the air hunting large moths. Sergei's comment comes into my head: the Afghan soldiers would shoot anything that moves. Perhaps the electronic barrier is working again, maybe they only turn it on at night. I manage to crawl as far as the bastion wall undetected, but in the darkness I can't find the rope. I crawl along the wall, cowering when I hear voices, I have to crawl back again, I have a panicked fear that I will be bitten by a snake. There are several species of venomous viper around here, sometimes they appear in the camp and trigger a panic. I grope my way along the wall and hope that in the end I will find the rope. At first, in my exhaustion I have to rest for a moment,

Nightjar (*Caprimulgus aegyptius*)

my head is spinning, the hours under the fierce sun have worn me out, I've lost too much water. The nightjars churr on and on in the darkness. I have the rope. I lie down on the top of the wall, lie there exhausted, until I hear the guards and jump down from the wall into the camp.

Sergei is still awake. He's been worried because I didn't come back to the container. Now I know it's possible to leave the camp undetected and return.

Sunday 3 August 2003

I've worked the whole evening in the sick bay. A vehicle from a convoy drove over a mine. No one was killed, but one soldier had his foot torn off. It's still stuck in his boot. His leg had to be amputated below the knee. When I get back to barracks, exhausted, Sergei is trying to speak to his wife again, but she isn't coming to the phone. His children tell him she's just gone to a neighbour's or to play sport or somewhere. Every time this happens Sergei ends up depressed. He senses that she doesn't want to speak to him. I try to console him, but he says he can't live without his wife, he would kill himself if she left him. We walk through the camp. I take him with me up on to the tower and show him the lake, the moonlight reflected in it. I tell Sergei about Theresa.

Tuesday 5 August 2003

Ramadan (they call it Ramzan here) has begun. Muslims eat, drink and smoke only when night falls, once they can no longer tell the difference between a white and a black thread. Especially devout Muslims regularly spit on the ground as well to show that they are not even swallowing their own spit. The camp is not attacked during this time, there aren't even incidents outside the camp, no one is expecting attacks. The native guards are less vigilant as a result. Ramadan will make my trip to the lake easier. Tomorrow I am going to try again – at last.

Wednesday 6 August 2003

I can't make out any guards in their tower, perhaps they're hunkered down behind the parapet, dozing. I scramble quickly over the Hesco wall, fasten my rope and lower myself down into the prohibited area, press myself against the wall in the blind spot, rest, gather my strength, the guards can't see me here. I run across the prohibited area to the fence, to the hole I dug on my first attempt. If they look in my direction, if the electronic barrier activates, it's all over. But no one notices me, perhaps the guards are asleep or drunk. Sergei has talked about them using alcohol and drugs when they're on duty. It doesn't matter to me what they're doing, all that matters is that they don't spot me or act as if they haven't. I slither through the hole under the fence and commando-crawl along to a dyke, I'm using every cover that's offered to me. The sun burns, there's no shade, in our container the intense heat had burst the thermometer again by mid-morning, sweat trickles down my neck, my body armour slips. I run along in a ditch behind the dyke, bent over. I'm so exhausted that I want nothing more than to drop to the ground. It takes much longer than I anticipated to get to the lake. At the shore a cooling wind blows. I flop down behind an old wall. No one can spy on me here, even with field binoculars. I glance at the lake. A sandbank, corrugated by the wind, stretches into the water. Plants grow on the lake shore, they resemble frogbit and spike-rush. I find the tracks of swifts, their feet, if you can call them feet, are stunted, and their prints look like holes, as if someone had pressed a marble into the mud. Their feet don't lend themselves to running. They hop about the place awkwardly. Swifts spend almost their entire lives in the air, only coming to the water to drink. When it rains, they gather the tiny water droplets that trickle down into their open beaks as they fly. But it hasn't rained for a month. Avocets lift off, wings refulgent white with flickering lines of black, elongated blue-grey legs, thin high whistles from their curved beaks as they fly away over my head.

Avocet (*Recurvirostra avosetta*)

Monday 11 August 2003

On Sunday I was at the lake again. It changes its colours constantly: one moment it is yellow ochre, the next it is like a mirror again, reflecting only the small islands of cloud high up in the sky. I sit on the wall, swallows skim over the water. I hear glittering notes, a blend of voices and noise. I believe that everything is made of one melody, which we are capable of hearing only at particular moments.

In the evening I try to call Theresa, but she doesn't pick up. It occurs to me that she can't make calls on the farm. She doesn't get around to writing after the strains of her working day, she often falls asleep at the kitchen table with fatigue.

In my dream I hear unknown, mellifluous bird calls again, but I am afraid that at some point that will change, and I will wake up screaming.

Theresa fried some bacon in the pan and then threw in the leftover pasta from yesterday. While Bruni was still working in the stable, Theresa sorted out the evening meal. Their food stocks were thoroughly depleted. Theresa added two more slices of cheese; now they had nothing else left except a packet of soup. They hadn't left the farm in a fortnight, slaving day after day in the stables and on the fields. Every evening she fell bone-weary into bed. Through the kitchen window Theresa could see a part of the stable and a stall lined with straw, on which a pregnant mare was standing. At night they had to keep watch over the mare, call the vet the moment she began to foal, there was no time to swim in the lake any longer, no more than to go into town to telephone Paul. Theresa sensed how much he needed her, needed someone he could talk to. During their last call she had told him that she had been with Jan and he was doing better, perhaps that helped. Kessler was standing with Bruni next to the mare, patting the horse's neck. She was an especially noble mare – ash-grey coat with a large white blaze and pale nostrils. Sometimes in the middle of the night the mare would kick with her hind legs against the wall behind which was Theresa's bed. Kessler's wife's Dalmatian ran restlessly back and forth between the stalls. After Kessler had left, Bruni mucked out the remaining stall. She was good with horses, she kept those stalls cleaner than her own room.

By the time Bruni came into the kitchen Theresa had prepared dinner and washed up the last few days' dishes. Bruni took off her dirty clothes, threw them into a corner and went for a shower. Theresa had to clear up everything after her. Later Bruni sat herself down at the table, her wet hair dripping. She wolfed down the pasta then rolled a cigarette and ranted about the mule, which stood with the horses in the paddock and bolted at every opportunity. Bruni fetched the bottle of schnapps from a kitchen cabinet, put it to her mouth and drained what was left in a single gulp. She leaned back, belched and plucked a thread of tobacco from her lips. Outside in the yard the Dalmatian was yelping. Suddenly Kessler was standing in the kitchen. Bruni had just put on her motorcycle helmet, they wanted to go shopping. Kessler told them they had to keep watch overnight and call the vet if things got started with the mare. 'We're going shopping now,' Bruni answered.

On the journey to the supermarket Theresa's mobile rang. It was in her rucksack, and she couldn't take the call. Perhaps it was Paul. She didn't much feel like talking to him.

In the supermarket they met the vet. He smiled at Theresa. They had run into each other in the café the last time she had visited Jan. The vet had told her he'd been covering for a colleague on an acute case at one of the estate farms. He'd invited her for a pizza and took her home afterwards. Bruni saw the look the vet threw Theresa in the supermarket. She sulked as she stuffed soup packets, ready meals and tins into her rucksack alongside pasta, bread and cheese. The people at the checkout wrinkled their noses because the smell of the stables still clung to their clothes. Outside Bruni pulled a bottle of whisky out from under her parka. 'Oops! I forgot to pay,' she laughed. They took a swig each and rode back to the farm.

Tuesday 12 August 2003

Assigned as medical support for mine-clearance duties. If it doesn't go pear-shaped, it's a nice enough job, I have all the time in the world to watch birds outside the camp. Some unexploded Russian rockets stuck in a field need to be defused and disposed of. After three hours on the road we arrive in the middle of the day. One of the bombs is rusted, it's impossible to unscrew the fuse, transporting it to the detonation site is too dangerous, so the platoon commander decides to blow it up *in situ*. While I'm sitting at a safe distance in the shade of a tree, the bomb-disposal experts are working in the fierce sun. Shortly before the detonation I spot a Güldenstädt's redstart (*Phoenicurus erythrogastus*), the top of its head and nape are light grey, its breast is tinted brown, its pinion feathers dazzle like polished glass. I try to scare it away because it's perched in a bush not very far from the bomb, the blast wave will tear it to pieces.

Wednesday 13 August 2003

I write to Jan about Nassim and my lake. Perhaps Odette will read it out to him. In our last phone call Theresa said he was going to be operated on again.

At night I hear bird calls and buzzing noises. I do not want to go mad. It consoles me to watch the birds, to see them in flight.

Nassim crouches behind the wall at the lake, smiles, as I sit myself down next to him, exhausted. He thinks I'm out of my mind coming here again and again. It's simpler than I thought, and now I can't stop myself.

When this war is finally over, Nassim hopes to obtain a German visa so that he can study there. He begs me to talk to him about Germany. It makes me realise how little I know about my country, that I've never figured out all the threads that led me here. Talking to him I feel as if I've lived until now on a planet entirely foreign to me.

This afternoon I watch red-necked grebes (*Podiceps grisegena*) in their nuptial plumage. They fly low over the lake with necks elongated and feet stretched out behind them, landing finally on the opposite shore in an area of shallow water. Their dark-brown crests reach as far as their eyes, and their partially extended head feathers give the impression of comical ear tufts.

Birds have the same multiplicity of colours as the things they see. Sometimes they vanish over the water, as if they have been conjured from our senses. Something vanished, which remains present. Perhaps reality is like that, and we will never grasp it, or perhaps there are also moments in which we understand things without knowing them.

Friday 15 August 2003

Sergei wants to go home, immediately, though he knows it's impossible. He has to wait until he gets his home leave. I try to calm him down. Sergei confides in me that the thought that his wife loves another man is driving him mad. We go to the bar with him, play table football and let him win. He drinks heavily and sometimes he spins his Rubik's Cube like a crazy man. Then he sits slumped on his bed again for hours at a time, tears running over his cheeks.

When I climb the tower in the evening, I spot Nassim, he's back by the lake, sitting on the remains of the wall. I lent him my binoculars. I'm sure he'll give them back because he knows how much they mean to me.

My journey has led me as far as these highlands, as far as the foot of prob-
ably the highest and noblest of mountains, with hills facing to the south
made of glittering white salts, merchant travellers come from all over,
even from the furthest provinces of China, to avail themselves of this pure
salt. Salt which appears as hard as diamantine stone, which only permits
itself to be broken with a steam hammer. The surrounding land is fruit-
ful, and in the city when I arrive a festival and a large grain market are
just then taking place. In the bazaar manifold birds are offered for sale,
birds with coloured plumage as if they have escaped from the Gardens of
Paradise. At the habitual times of migration the farmers, it seems, capture
the most gifted in speech amongst these journeymen of the air. Goldfinches,
red-fronted serins, calandra larks, red-headed buntings, waxwings, rock
nuthatches, hoopoes, mynahs and many more. From my spot in the shade
afforded by an acacia, I am able to witness a quail fight in the bazaar. The
small, delicate birds have had their wings clipped. They whet their little
yellow beaks on the withies of their cages. A cloth is spread out in that very
place in the dust to form the arena for the fight. The proud owners take
their savage little birds carefully out of their cages, chafe them in their
hands to bring them to a sweat and build their lust for battle. Wagers as
to which of the noble little birds will in the end be the victor are swiftly
concluded. Meanwhile pewter sand trickles from a glowing glass flask
into the wrinkled hand of an old man, who appears to count each single
tiny grain. The cheap fights mostly end without bloodshed, as the defeated
quail quits the field.

I saw human creatures skilled in flight, men with artificial pinions,
who could soar high above in the azure sea of air like eagles.

Wednesday 20 August 2003

Sergei is on home leave. Thank God, as it was barely endurable, he was just crucifying himself. I hope a solution presents itself for the difficulties with his wife. For now I'm living in the dormitory only with Julian, though probably not for much longer because Julian has volunteered for a mission that requires snipers.

In the evening I draw up a list of the birds I've seen at the lake. Sergei calls from Germany, he's moaning, he's sitting alone in an empty house, his wife has left him and taken the kids, why, he doesn't know, he doesn't even have a bed and has to sleep on the bare floor, worse than in the camp.

Friday 22 August 2003

Back at the lake at last, I immediately take off my uniform, lie down in the shade and listen in to the polyphonic song of the birds. Perhaps Ambrosius was right after all: there is a language of birds, they can communicate with each other in ways we cannot comprehend. I think of Theresa, I imagine that she is here beside me.

Today the lake appears an opal green, veiled by haze, in the middle the water is dark, a sign of unfathomable depths, like the Schalkenmehrener and Gemündener maars back home. Pond skaters create small glittering dots as they move. I stay as long as I can, run back to the camp in the twilight, crawl the last section up to the fence, scramble under it and climb over the Hesco wall with my rope before roll call. I won't be able to get to the lake again because the current guards are being replaced tomorrow.

Sunday 24 August 2003

I lie on my bed and read as Julian meticulously packs his rucksack. He'll be spending the coming weeks at a small remote outpost. It's a dangerous mission. His squad are to protect a village from Taliban attacks. A total of ten soldiers will be stationed there, living in trenches and tents on a knoll outside the village.

I'll miss Julian, even though he's been getting on my nerves a lot lately. Every time I've come back from one of my excursions to the lake, he's wanted to know where I was. Now that Julian is gone and I have so much more freedom, I can't just leave the camp without thinking about it any longer. I have no information about the watch schedules. It would be smarter to wait until Sergei is back from leave before my next excursion. Smartest of all would be to drop something so completely insane. I am afraid that central command will at some point notice that the electronic barrier isn't working or change the watch schedule without me knowing.

Monday 25 August 2003

It is yawningly boring in the camp. I'm glad when the opportunity arises to go out on a patrol and give myself something else to think about. We travel for five hours to a hillside village comprised of numerous simple mud huts. In the valley a plain covered in low bushes stretches out. The sappers are surveying a plot of land on the edge of the village which is meant to serve as the site of a school for girls. While they work I crouch down in the shade of a wall and look out over the valley. Around fifty northern lapwings (*Vanellus vanellus*) are gathered in a field. Nassim has still not given me back my binoculars, so I have to make do with the military binoculars. I don't see Nassim any more. I don't know what's going on with him. He no longer appears to be working at the camp. Through the military binoculars I see less, or differently, they simply aren't my father's binoculars. The lapwings lift off from the field with loose, leisurely wing beats, fly in elegant zigzags swaying and swinging up and down with their wings like curved paddles. With their black upper sides gleaming in the sunlight and the black-white of their bellies I can make them out easily. Their heads are white with black foreheads, ending in a long, two-pointed crest. A black band with blurred edges runs from their beak under each eye towards the back of the head.

Northern lapwing (*Vanellus vanellus*)

Today one of our armoured recce vehicles ran into a booby trap while crossing a bridge. The driver bought it, the other soldiers survived with minor injuries, because the driver's body absorbed the force of the explosion.

By the time I arrive with the captain at the ambulance that has brought the dead man back to camp, the door is already open. We climb into the vehicle, inside the heat is overpowering. Mechanically I fold back the sheet, which has been spread over the dead man, and unbutton his uniform so that the doctor can conduct his examination. Suddenly I am holding warm intestines in my hands. I push them back into the abdomen, wipe my hands and note down the injuries on a pad as the captain dictates his examination. After we've completed our work, the soldier is taken to the cold store.

In the night I hear a buzzing tangle of bird calls, I see Jan as he lay on the forest floor after the accident, his face streaming with blood, how he suddenly opened his eyes, stared at me and gave out a marrow-shaking laugh. I wake up soaked in sweat, the only sound I can hear is the noise of the air conditioning. I walk outside, sit down in front of the container and cry.

When Jan woke up out of his coma, he could no longer speak. He didn't remember anything, not even that I had been driving the car. The tyres had simply slid on the muddy forest floor, the brakes didn't bite, the Rover flipped over, I was flung from the vehicle. Then the car rammed one pine tree after another, careering along on its roof and smashing into a thick tree trunk. I staggered through the forest, saw a rescue helicopter high above the treetops, blacked out and woke up in a hospital somewhere.

Wednesday 27 August 2003

Now in the height of summer the water level in the lake is dropping. Each time I look out over it from the tower it's withdrawn a little further, like a snail creeping back into its shady home. I'm watching out for Nassim, hoping I'll spot him at the lake. He hasn't been to work in the camp for weeks. Perhaps he's taken up his studies again, or else he's fallen ill.

In the evening, tremors from an earthquake. We are used to them by now. But this time the epicentre is nearer than most of the other quakes I've experienced so far. Just as I bolt out of my container into the open air, it is over. I can't go back to sleep and walk to the bar, where I play table football the whole night. There are smaller aftershocks, every time I laugh like a lunatic as the ball hops on the pitch.

The camp is under rocket attack several times a week, the guards have been reinforced and are in a state of constant alert. It is misty and oppressive, like in a steam room. I have a fever. With the strengthening of the guard it's impossible to climb over the Hesco wall unnoticed or make it across the prohibited area. I watch how my lake steams in the blazing sun, I fear it will soon dry out completely. I dream I am standing in the middle of the parched lake bed, Nassim is waiting there for me. No one in the camp can tell me where he is. Back in the container I keep the doors and windows closed so that the temperature stays at least halfway bearable.

I've heard nothing from Theresa. I write letters and then tear them up moments later. When I last spoke to my mother she didn't know anything about Theresa. My mother announced that she is going to marry again. She actually asked me what I thought about that. I indicated that it was of no interest to me, I don't know her husband-to-be and she should do what she wants to do, just as she has always done.

Saturday 30 August 2003

Back then I soared like a bird in my dreams. When I was a child I crafted a flying suit for myself like Ambrosius by sewing the feathers of hawks, rooks, carrion crows, eagle owls, doves, jays, buzzards, falcons, magpies on to a gauze. I stood with my flying suit on the roof of the shed and waited for a favourable wind, updraughts that would raise me high into the air, as if in a lift. I wanted to be a magpie. It senses the wind with its white chest, then pushes off and begins to scull. To this day I think I would have been able to fly if only I had been light enough.

On Sunday morning I wake up on my camp bed surrounded by the countless feathers I have collected out here. I am frightened because I have no memory of scattering them on my bed.

Suddenly I am standing in the searchlights, I feel like an enraged, dangerous animal, the entire prohibited area is brightly lit, sirens wail, evidently the photoelectric sensor has been repaired in the last few days. The guards have been alerted, they've spotted me, levelled their rifles at me. They'd no longer be able to let me go, even if they wanted to. It is like in a fever dream. I don't know what I was doing the whole of Sunday before I climbed into the prohibited area, probably I just lay on my bed and dreamed of the lake. I know I tried to reach Theresa, but it was impossible to get a connection. They take me to the sick bay. The camp commander is informed of the incident. I am brought to him and have to justify myself to him. I climbed over the Hesco wall, I explain, because I saw a goatsucker from the tower. This sounds so insane that the commander gives the appearance of being interested, or at any rate lets me finish speaking. I tell him about my interest in ornithology, I discourse on this bird, that it is also called nightjar, that it hatches its eggs on the ground and sleeps during the day on the branches of trees. I refer to Pliny the Elder, who describes the goatsucker in his *Naturalis Historia*. Supposedly this bird sucked the milk from goats by night, which would turn them blind or kill them. In reality, however, the goatsucker was enticed by the insects that accompany pastoral animals. I noticed from the tower, I say, that the bird was injured. The commander listens attentively, but I can see in his face that he doesn't take me seriously. He smiles and says that I ought to care more for the health of my comrades. Eventually he asks what in my opinion our purpose is for being here. I answer exactly as we were told: we are defending the freedom of this country and the freedom of the Western world. I get three days' detention, in which I have to write a report on obedience and orders, I have to complete fourteen additional days' medical administrative duties and pay a 1,000-euro fine, which will be taken from my pay. The punishment is lenient because I have been, until now, a good soldier.

I was sixteen years old when my father began to train again. Mother had not been living with us for several months. I was already by then almost as tall as my father and just as lanky. His love for the world of birds I had inherited, his enthusiasm for the high jump, not at all.

Mother had gone because she had fallen in love with another man. For several months she lived with her boyfriend in Cologne and worked as a waitress in a restaurant in the old city. She only telephoned my father occasionally, and it was always about money, all she wanted to know about us children was how we were doing at school. My sister refused to speak to her. Once, when my dad wanted to give her the handset, she ran out of the house, through our garden, across a field of horses and right through the village as far as a large cornfield, where she hid herself and stayed out all night.

My father had never envisaged my mother might leave him, it was completely unimaginable for him. They had known each other since school. He had courted her for a long time, until eventually she had married him. One evening he fetched his old training schedules out of a box in the loft and studied them. Next day, after his shift at the cement works, he drove to the athletics ground in Kall. I spotted him there when the school bus drove past at lunchtime. Father sprinted, made an elegant standing jump over the bar and landed softly on the mats, which he had brought out of the gymnasium by himself. That my father was now tackling the high jump again, I interpreted as a diversion, to stop him having to think about Mother. At the time, it was better he was doing sport rather than starting to drink or something else completely mad. I was sure that at some point he would stop jumping again. But father didn't stop, not even after Mother had come back, because the man who had lured her away left her six months later. One day she was standing there at the sports ground with her suitcase, sat herself down on the bench in front of the small terrace, built on a mound of earth, and watched my father, who was training on the other side of the football pitch. Father was by this time already jumping over two metres again, using his own variant of the Fosbury Flop. He ran at the jump not exactly square on, but rather along the track he himself had set up, parallel to the jump, shortly before take-off he sprinted up to the bar at an oblique angle, pivoted on his own axis at the moment of take-off and rotated himself upwards into a supine position. The final two steps were significantly shorter – he planted in them all the energy of his run-up. At the moment of take-off Father stretched both his arms up high and, as he pivoted, his fingertips touched the 'magic bar', an imaginary barrier at two metres high, over which he wanted to fly. When my father talked about the high jump, he only ever spoke of flying, at some point during your flight you reach the moment from which the fall begins. The distinction between jumping, flying and falling was only one of time, and time was relative, sometimes seconds felt to us like hours. He said, 'If you want to jump high, really high, you have to forget time and simply want to keep on flying.'

Mother clapped when Father cleared the bar. For the first time he saw her, sitting on the bench. She'd lost weight, had cut her hair short and dyed it. He could make out a small tattoo on her neck, a scorpion, not particularly conspicuous, barely as big as a thumbnail. Father had known she would come back sometime. He didn't walk over to her, he carried on training instead.

Later, when Mother was living with us again, they no longer spoke to one another, at least nothing that was relevant. Father no longer looked at her because of that strange tattoo. I don't know what he was thinking as he sat on the motorway bridge in the evenings and watched the peregrine falcons, but at some point he must have had the idea of risking the jump. After my mother came back my sister moved out, lived with friends, abandoned school and began to take drugs. Sometimes she spent the whole night cruising around the neighbourhood on her scooter. I bumped into her now and again at the parties that used to be held in an old factory building in Zingsheim. We barely spoke to each other, you couldn't have a sensible conversation with her any more, at most she asked what Dad was up to, stammered incoherently and disappeared with some young guy.

In the early summer the peregrine falcons raised another clutch. This time all three nestlings survived. My father told us how he watched them on their first flight. The young birds stayed in the territory for a few weeks after they had fledged and then left. They lay in wait somewhere along the coast for migrating birds or moved to southern or eastern Europe.

Whenever my father talked about his bird-watching, my mother would stand up, wordlessly leave the kitchen and then put the television on loud in the lounge. I believe my mother had intended to change when she came back to us. But my father took no notice of her, didn't talk to her, and when he came home from work occupied himself entirely with his birds and the high jump.

During the winter months Father trained in the sports hall. Because the hall was too small for his old jumping technique he had to reorganise once again and make do with a shorter run-up. At home he watched videos for hours, studied freeze frames showing how birds took off from the ground or from branches. There are some species of bird, magpies and jays, for example, which need a long run-up to get themselves into the air, and with these birds flight always consists of constant rising and falling. Perhaps when he jumped my father imagined himself flying as a magpie flew. Mother began to meet up with other men again. She didn't do it secretly any more, on the contrary, everyone knew, though Father seemed to take no interest in any of it. One morning in early summer, I had wanted to set out for school first thing, and my father's training shoes were no longer sitting on the shelf next to our front door. He had jogged as far as the bridge. By then he was very fit and could jump high.

Thursday 11 September 2003

Every day I carry out my medical duties, and every day they hit me with extra tasks. Amongst others, I have to conduct a comprehensive stocktake of our medical equipment and drugs.

I have spoken once briefly with Theresa, told her about my attempt to make my way to the lake and that I got caught. She doesn't understand me. I say to her that I can hardly sleep and am sweating incessantly and dreaming things for which I can find no explanation. I have told her that I think of her often.

With the heightened alert of the guards and the electronic barriers working again, it's impossible to climb over the Hesco wall unobserved and make it across the prohibited area. The alarm, which is triggered by the smallest movement, has become a catastrophe for the Afghan foxes and birds. The guards are under strict orders to shoot at anything loitering in the prohibited area. From my tower I can see the cadaver of a fox, see how the lake is evaporating in the burning sun. Of Nassim, no trace.

Saturday 20 September 2003

No more punishment duties at last. In recent weeks I've become a nothing, I've spent my days and late into the nights on the wards and in the ambulance. But in some ways it's done me good. I have been asking about Nassim too often. Which is probably the reason I am summoned to the company commander, who interrogates me about Nassim and my sexual orientation. He has my files and Nassim's on the table in front of him. Nassim has formally given his notice in order to resume his studies, the commander explains. I tell him about Theresa, who is waiting for me back home. It comes easily to me to offer up this fairy tale – after all, it is what I most want to be true. The company commander looks as if he believes me. On the basis of which I end up requesting that I be allowed to go out on missions again.

In the evening, Sergei calls from Germany. He cries and says he's not allowed to see his children, he's living in a shabby hotel room, spends most of his time roaming the city alone. Sergei wants to come back. I don't tell him I got caught on one of my excursions, and I don't mention Nassim and the interrogation.

Helena had been reading and sorting papers the whole afternoon. She had been down to the kitchen only once briefly, brewed herself a cup of tea then climbed back up the stairs to the room that she now only ever called her 'story room'. She stood at the window and watched the deer grazing at the edge of the forest; they always ventured out from amongst the pines at dusk. Sometimes they lifted their heads and looked anxiously around, vanished with long strides into the forest and after a little while came back to their feeding ground. Helena was doing better now, she was even doing some exercise. She had met up with Leo in the meantime as well. They had arranged to meet in a hotel room in Cologne. After they had slept together, she had told Leo that she could no longer meet him, that she had to forget him, even if that was impossible. She examined one of Paul's bird drawings thoughtfully, one of the watercolours that had run and blurred with the wet; it was hard for her to make out what bird it represented. Helena thought of her former pupil, saw him in front of her, how he had sat proudly enthroned on top of her teacher's desk and read out his essay on the world of birds. She remembered another boy from back then, though he had never been her pupil, who had pressed his mucky face against the windowpane from outside and watched what was going on in the room. The classroom was on the second floor, the boy must have shinned up the drainpipe and somehow clung on to the window ledge. He had his nose pressed flat against the glass. She could not make out the features of his face exactly, except for his spherical, curious, light-blue eyes, which seemed to be searching for something in the classroom, something unattainable for him. When the boy thought he had been spotted, he jumped down into the bushes. She had walked over to the window, watched how he had limped across the cloister garden and climbed over the wall, behind which lay the street, leading down to the children's home.

At her most recent check-up, as she was walking across the hospital car park with Ignatz, she had involuntarily glanced up at the window where Paul had been standing. The lady at reception had informed her that there was no Paul Arimond here, quite definitely no one like that on any of the wards in the hospital, perhaps he had already been discharged or relocated, no more details were available. She had been satisfied with this information and made no further enquiries. She was glad that things were going better for her, the doctor had not found any new metastases. Ignatz had waited for her outside in the car, afterwards they had driven home and that evening for the first time in a long time, they had slept together.

When Ignatz came home from work, it was already dark and the deer had disappeared again into the forest. Ignatz knew that Helena wanted her quiet. He prepared dinner, carried it up to her and put fresh flowers in the vase. Then he left her alone again, went downstairs, turned the television on and watched, as always at that time of day, the news. The war in Afghanistan was becoming ever more dangerous.

Only a few sheets of paper still lay on the floor in front of Helena, sheets she could not fully decipher and which often described tangled, peculiar and terrible things. She had bought a portfolio and filed away the remaining pages into it. She sat herself down on the floor and read.

Tuesday 23 September 2003

Sergei has been back from leave since yesterday. I'm really happy to have him back in our dorm. We hug and spend the whole night talking. He tells me that his wife met some other guy and is now living with her kids at her new boyfriend's place. He tries to talk about it in a clinical way, as he perches on his bed and spins his cube, lightning fast he's solved it and tosses it to me to jumble it up again. I know he doesn't want to force his unhappiness on me. He asks after Julian, who is still deployed on a hill watching over a site at the edge of Taliban-controlled territory.

In the evening we go to the bar and play table football against the new arrivals. It's the first time I've been back there in a long while. After my attempt to get out of the camp got around my comrades have kept their distance.

After Ambrosius returned to the village, he is said to have retreated into his cottage by the river and begun to construct a flying machine, an ornithopter. Perhaps he thought that humans would only be able to understand the birds and their language once they, like the birds, had soared free and weightless in the sky. He believed that birds had roads in the air similar to those that men had on the ground, paths upon which wind currents led them into the heavens. Thus it was vital to pay close attention to the wind, you had to jump with your flying machine at the right moment on to one of these wind paths, then you would be borne up into the sky automatically, as if on a litter. The air was composed of an invisible, incessantly shifting tangle of roads, paths and tracks, a labyrinth in which the birds found their way. Ambrosius is said to have compiled a map of the wind paths to a radius of ten kilometres around our village. He claimed that a human being is a bird that is no longer able to fly, because a bird without feathers had a form akin to a naked, bent-over human; by the same token, our hair consisted, like bird feathers, of creatine, and our speech had merely unlearned how to sing.

Father sat with me on the spot where Ambrosius had sat back then, watching the rooks in flight, on a treeless hill on the edge of our village that we named Sky-Mountain. We perched up there on a cattle trough and looked down into the Boletal, tracked the crows floating over the hillside as they taught their young how to fly in the sea of air. Ambrosius, it is said, completed his ornithopter one day. He took the proportions of his own body and the wings of various species of bird as a basis and calculated a wing area of 126 square feet. This area was, by his calculations, necessary for a man of his size and weight to be carried by the wind. The pinions were made of the tanned skins of fire salamanders, which the children of the village had caught for him. The women of the village sewed the individual skins together into a large flight skin – pinions three metres in length, light as a feather, thin and translucent as parchment. Ambrosius, it is said, fastened the pinions to his scrawny old man's arms with leather thongs and steered the tail feathers of his ornithopter with his feet. He was by then a very old man, ate next to nothing for months beforehand to make himself exceptionally light. Then he waited on the hill for the wind, the wind that ought to come past with the migrating birds, sometimes his wings billowed out and his feet lifted a few centimetres off the pasture, he flapped his arms, floated back and forth a little, but no one believed that he could really fly. One morning after a stormy night Ambrosius was no longer on the mountain. When the villagers looked up into the sky, they believed they could see him floating there, carried on the updraughts, spiralling higher and higher, until he vanished in the heavens.

Wednesday 24 September 2003

We rise at daybreak, pack our equipment and walk to our vehicles. I'm glad to be heading out of the camp again, even if I know neither the destination nor the purpose of our mission.

Our armoured personnel carrier rumbles over pot-holed tarmac. It is hot. I look out of the hatch. Cornfields gleam and sway in the sun, always between them banks and ditches of clay, low bushes and isolated trees with short narrow trunks, coated in fine, ochre-coloured dust. I watch a Barbary falcon (*Falco pelegrinoides*) over a patch of field. It is more or less the size of a crow, its crown and nape are rust-coloured, its coat of feathers is grey-blue, just like its big brother the peregrine falcon. By the side of the road there are kilometres of shattered ruins and wrecked Russian tanks. Sergei is sitting next to me. Suddenly I hear birds again, I would love to talk about them with someone.

We pass through villages of dilapidated, clay-coloured hovels, children wave at us from the side of the road, we drive onwards on sandy tracks, stop, dismount, take a pee and have a smoke. The landscape becomes hillier, better watered, green. I glance from our vehicle into a narrow valley, on to dense treetops, soon we are again crossing the steppe, then we are going steadily uphill. Because we haven't completed our route in a single day, we stop on elevated ground and secure our camp, arranging the vehicles in a circle and making our weapon systems combat ready.

Lying under an outstretched mosquito net, I look at the starry sky. Since I've been here, I have become ever more of a riddle to myself, but I am in some peculiar way happy. I think of Ambrosius and his journey through this country.

I wake very early and hear birds twittering, as if voices and songs were answering each other. We set off on our journey back to camp without having accomplished any task that I can make out. Yesterday, however, in the late afternoon, during a rest stop, I did for the first time see Himalayan snowcocks (*Tetraogallus himalayensis*), large swift-gliding birds that resemble our capercaillies.

Himalayan snowcock (*Tetraogallus himalayensis*)

Thursday 2 October 2003

Yesterday a letter came from Theresa. She writes about visiting Jan. He's making great progress since his last operation and learning to speak again. Theresa read my letters out to Jan. Odette handed them over to her and asked her to send me her regards. Theresa tells me about the arduous work on the farm, about her scarce free time and Kessler's refusal to give her the weekends off. She talks about the vet, who she now refers to by his first name. Justus, she writes, has invited her for something to eat and to go to the cinema. She has bumped into my mother in the supermarket in Kall. Mother complained to her that I don't telephone her often enough. Then she writes that if we want to meet up when I get back, we could go together to visit Jan. She worries about me. She has enclosed a four-leafed clover with the letter, and the alula feather of a jay, with its bands of black and pale blue.

Monday 6 October 2003

I sit on the rear bench of the armoured vehicle, watch the world around us through the dusty pane of the small window, look at the fields, bushes and copses, narrow, dried-out irrigation ditches. We're travelling to a small village. Our engineers have a mission to pull down the curtain wall of a bridge that crosses an irrigation ditch into the village. After that the bridge is supposed to be widened. While the construction squad begins to demolish the concrete bridge with pneumatic hammers, we secure our vehicles parked in the village square and look out over the street from the armoured personnel carrier.

When we get back from our mission in the evening, I am exhausted. I actually have more feathers, enough by now to fill a crate, which I want to clean and stick into an album. But instead I lie down on my bed, read Theresa's letter another time, she writes that she has quarrelled with Bruni, Bruni is jealous of her because of Justus, though she has no reason to be. I fall asleep as I'm reading and wake up again very early, shower and then walk to the canteen. Levier has forgotten to tie up his shoes again, shuffles with his tray from the counter to the table in the corner, parks his tray on the table, braces himself with the heels of his hands against the edge of the table and stares dead ahead, sunk in thought and breathing heavily. At moments it looks like he's talking to someone or having a conversation with himself. He stands there like that for a while, then sits down and starts to leaf through his papers.

Rockets are fired at us almost every night, they fly over the camp and explode in the fields.

Tuesday 14 October 2003

Several government soldiers have been killed in a Taliban attack on an army lorry. A girls' school has been burned to the ground. There have been multiple rocket attacks on an outpost of coalition troops in Khost, a province in eastern Afghanistan. We hear nothing of the dead and wounded or the identity of the attackers.

It is dark and quiet in the room, the only sounds are Sergei's shallow breathing and the unchanging buzzing noise of the air conditioner. I fall asleep, wake up straight away soaked in sweat, remember my dream. Our patrol has broken into a windowless hovel, the occupants are naked and stink of excrement. I am trying desperately to remove mites from their eyes with a pair of tweezers, but I cannot help them. Outside in the darkness they are leaping around a fire, arms flailing. Then they are skewering birds on to a stick, burning away the plumage, roasting them over the fire, tearing at the flesh with their filthy teeth and gulping it down. They are mating with white winged creatures like vultures, they feed on the filth from a vast rubbish heap. Sergei thinks these dreams are nothing unusual and will disappear eventually, I will forget them.

The sun's rays fall through the window into the container. I hear my heart beating and see my life flying away. For a moment I am looking into Jan's eyes, as if he is bent right over me, and I feel his breath, smell it. I call his name, wake in panic.

Saturday 18 October 2003

We are three again in the container, Julian is back from his mission. He tells us about driving past vast poppy fields, of mice and rats in the boggy dugout where they all lived together. The mice even crawled into his sleeping bag. He dreamed of having a shower almost every night.

Julian has brought me back feathers, tries to describe the birds he saw through his telescopic sight on guard duty. He has changed, he no longer has his old confidence in his future, at night I hear him sobbing. One time he tells us about looking out over a field from their hill. In the middle of the field was a small boy on a raised platform chasing away the crows with clattering tin cans.

For weeks the boy was sat there for the whole day, he was a living scarecrow. In the morning at the crack of dawn he clambered up on to the platform and only went back to his village at dusk. Julian almost cries as he tells us this. Something must have happened, Julian's hands tremble.

Sunday 19 October 2003

Yesterday evening after Julian found out about my unauthorised excursion from our comrades in the bar, he berates me. He's drunk, comes into our dorm, says nothing at first, eyes me warily. Then he screams at me, have I lost my mind? He doesn't want to share a room with someone who could destroy his career. The lieutenant has already asked him whether he knew anything about it, reminded him that he is obliged to report any incidents like this. He rips my drawing from my hand, screws it into a ball and throws it in the corner. 'You think you're something better than us because you make crap like that.' We argue, eventually we fight. Julian is much stronger. I am lying beneath him, and he is just about to hit me again when Sergei arrives and separates us. My lip is bleeding.

Monday 20 October 2003

It's autumn, the change of season starts later here, but it happens more quickly than back home. I've accompanied several patrols over the last few weeks. The fields have been harvested. Unlike in our country the sacks of crops are left out in the fields for a long time because there's no rain now until shortly before the first snowfall. We distribute winter clothing in the surrounding villages and suspend our mobile clinics. It's going to be a cold winter. At the request of my captain I have had to defer my leave again, there are too few experienced medics in the battalion right now. I'd been looking forward to seeing Theresa again.

On our last patrol I saw the following species: bar-tailed treecreepers, black-crested tits, paradise fly-catchers, slaty-headed parakeets, Himalayan bulbuls, rose-ringed parakeets, pheasant-tailed jacanas, sunbirds, Himalayan woodpeckers and Indian lesser spotted woodpeckers.

There've been no rocket attacks for a week. It seems that the closer winter gets, the more the Taliban are concerned with their own survival.

Wednesday 5 November 2003

Demoiselle cranes (*Anthropoides virgo*) are heading south to their wintering grounds. They fly over our camp. I watch them high above us, soaring past in the direction of the Hindu Kush like delicate filaments. Some of them rest at the lake before crossing the vast mountain chain. With my military binoculars I've seen them glide in low over the water and land with supreme elegance, grand, beautiful wading birds. Their body feathers, the upper and lower coverts as well as the axillary feathers, are blue-grey, their secondaries are shiny black, the elbow feathers are smoky grey with dark tips. Behind their red-brown eyes runs a crescent-shaped tuft of narrow white feathers, which gives them a very distinguished appearance. They spend the night with their long legs standing in shallow water so that foxes and martens don't disturb their sleep. During the day they search for sustenance on the harvested fields nearby, returning to the lake each evening. Then, one morning, they resume their migration, lifting off with ease and grace. A long, gruelling path lies ahead of them, winter is approaching. Cranes are said to bring luck, but I don't know what kind of luck it's meant to be.

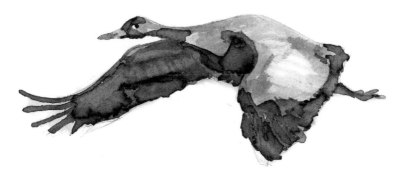

Demoiselle crane (*Anthropoides virgo*)

Friday 28 November 2003

It's gone cold, the temperature drops in the night to minus twenty degrees. We haven't left the camp for three weeks. Last week the heating wasn't working. I shivered the whole night under the blanket and thought about Theresa. I hope her heating is working again.

One morning I finally sighted my fifth species of magpie, several superb exemplars of the species *Pica pica hemileucoptera*. According to Ambrosius, their range is central Siberia: the Sayan Mountains, northwest Mongolia, Turkestan, western Tian Shan, the Talas Alatau range and the Altai Mountains. They perch on our antenna systems and satellite dishes. It's so cold I can barely hold on to my binoculars. I have to take off my gloves to adjust them. But at last I have them in front of me, close up and entirely clear. This species is larger than *Pica pica bactriana*, with glittering green secondaries, the tail is yellow and the primaries don't have the black markings you find in the other species. I wait for them to show me some aerobatics, but they prefer to just sit there and palaver.

I've been writing most of my entries in the library recently, even when it's been very cold there. I've been trying to write a letter to Theresa.

Bruni had fitted the stallion into his bridle, was attempting to lead him into the horsebox, but he didn't seem to want to be parted from the mule. He had bucked, kicked, eventually broken free and run through the open stable door into the yard. Now he was trotting restlessly along the path that led to the yard gate and which resembled an ice rink of frozen snow, shining in the sun. Bruni had to take care with every step not to slip over and land on her backside. The stallion pranced back and forth, its head held high, its dark skin glittering in the sun. Bruni tried again to grab him by the bridle, but it would have been better if she had waited until he had calmed down. As Bruni neared the animal, he ran from her, his hooves skidded away from him; for a moment he looked like a dancer who has lost his balance, then he was lying on his side, legs pedalling air, he got back up, ran in panic along the path past the stables towards the manor house and back again. Bruni followed him; he kicked out, catching her on the leg. Theresa, who had been watching the scene from the house, ran over to the entrance to the yard and pulled the gate shut. The stallion charged down the path towards her, a crazed look flickered in his eyes, and he whinnied in fear. Theresa was afraid he would run her over. 'Stop him!' yelled Bruni. But Theresa ducked at the last moment, as the stallion jumped clean over her and the gate in one huge leap and set off down the slope of the steep entrance way. She had never seen a horse jump so high or so far, it wasn't really a jump any more, the stallion had taken off and hovered in the air. The stallion landed on the glassy smooth village road, skidded down the slope like an unsteady skater, toppled over, turned over several times, got back up on its legs and hurtled off at a gallop.

Bruni hobbled over to the fence. She shoved Theresa aside. 'That was completely your fault,' she shouted. Her trousers were soaked in blood from where she had been kicked. 'I thought he was going to break every bone in his body on the ice,' said Bruni. 'One more piece of luck for you.' Theresa ran to the manor house and rang the bell for Kessler. She waited in the doorway. Since she'd been working at the farm, she had only once been inside the house, in the large living room where an open fire burned and the Kesslers received their riding guests and customers. Theresa waited until Kessler had pulled on a jumper and a jacket. He cursed constantly, lamented that he didn't know what to do with them. 'Why didn't you spread some salt?' Kessler shouted. When they stepped into the chilly kitchen, Bruni was sitting at the table, she had pulled her trousers down to her calves, her leg was swollen. 'The stupid bitch let him jump over the gate,' she moaned. Theresa ran with Kessler to the four-by-four; he threw the junk from the passenger seat into the back, and she sat down next to him. They drove around for the whole night until finally in the dawn light, they spotted the stallion in a meadow near the maar. He had scratches on his cheeks and he was limping, but he didn't run away when Theresa approached, talking to him in a soothing voice, put him into the bridle and led him to the horsebox. Justus came in the early morning to look at the injured animal. Theresa held the stallion still in the horsebox as Justus treated his wounds and examined him. When Justus had gone, she wept.

Wednesday 10 December 2003

Levier is standing in front of me in the canteen, his hands are shaking, I'm afraid that in the next moment everything he's loaded up on to his tray will fall to the floor. When he lifts his beret, I realise that his smooth-shaven skull has been painted an electric blue. He stares at me as if he's seeing me here in the canteen for the first time, suddenly yells, 'Attention!' I click my heels together, salute and walk to my table. I can hear him conducting his soliloquy, some of the time he whispers softly, then he is shouting, as if he wants to berate himself. Other people must notice how he's behaving, how he looks. Perhaps I should report his conduct to my captain.

Monday 22 December 2003

A few days before Christmas, and it has started to snow. I stand on the tower in the evening, looking out towards the lake, where I have not been since they caught me. If I made another attempt and got caught, I'd be sent home and demoted. If there were any possibility of making it to the lake, I believe I would have taken it. But I'm a prisoner in the camp now. The lake is unreachable and, like the rest of the countryside, covered in snow. Perhaps it doesn't even exist any more, perhaps it's disappeared like Nassim suddenly disappeared.

Two of our soldiers were injured in an attack on a convoy, one of them seriously. After emergency care in our field hospital, he was flown by helicopter to the larger medical facility at the main camp in Mazar-i-Sharif.

It snows continuously now. White-flecked Afghan foxes in their winter coats play in the fields in front of the fence. From the tower I watch a group of my comrades leave the bar, happy and elated. They stomp through the freshly fallen snow and shove each other into the white wetness, lying on their backs they flail their arms and legs, sculpting snow angels. I don't go to the bar any more. My comrades can no longer tolerate me, nor I them. Sergei is in the group. He knows that I'm standing up on the tower and glances furtively up at me.

Today at midday I telephoned Mother – as ever she didn't have much time while she's working. I ask about Theresa, but she hasn't heard or seen anything of her. My mother always complains that I rarely call her, but when I do speak to her she hardly says anything. 'Nothing much has happened at our end,' is all she says. I tell her how boring and cold it is here. She says that the marten we trapped before has come back. Every morning, when she starts her car to drive down the mountain into Kall, she's afraid that it will have gnawed through the brake pipe. She's planning to set the traps again. At night she can hear it scratching and scrabbling under the roof.

Tuesday 6 January 2004

I clamber up the tower and watch ravens romping in the blue sky. They are the most accomplished aerial acrobats I know. The icy temperatures appear to have no effect on them. They roll over jauntily in the air and fly for a while on their backs. The fun they're having is unmistakeable. One raven has a branch in its beak, the others are trying to snatch it away. As they play their games, they remind me of children jumping to dizzy heights on some vast trampoline. In stormy weather, when the other birds hide themselves away, the ravens dance in the air. I think of how I used to watch the crows from the Sky-Mountain with my dad, sitting on the trough, how he told me about Ambrosius's adventures and the people with zephyr souls.

With this volume of snow we can't get to the hospital on the edge of the city, can't hold our usual clinic there. Instead we shovel snow several times a day, in order to keep the pathways clear at least. In the classrooms it's pleasantly warm. Julian sits in the front row. He pretends to be interested, even in topics where he definitely knows much more than the instructor. I sit next to Sergei in the back row, sometimes I doze off with boredom. There are moments when, half asleep, I hear the birds singing with voices I've never heard before. I think of my schooldays, how I sat in the classroom with Jan and looked out into the cloister garden. Sergei prods me, makes me look outside at Levier, who is stumbling through the snow to the canteen wearing only his underwear.

In the evenings I go with Sergei to the camp cinema or we play table football. Most of the time though I sit alone in the container and work on my books of feathers. I'm sorry I can't show them to Nassim. More and more often I'm woken in the night by the voices of birds. My fellow soldiers avoid me, they whisper about me behind my back, to my face they ostentatiously talk through me as if I'm not there at all.

Tuesday 13 January 2004

I accompany a convoy on a mission to repair a faulty radio station. During the journey my fellow soldiers whisper about Levier. I find out that he's not been in the camp for the last three days. I saw him in the canteen last week, I'd already got used to his strange behaviour. 'You wouldn't be normal, if you didn't go mad here at some point,' says one of my comrades. Levier was taken away secretly one morning, on what grounds exactly, no one knows.

We travel for four hours over snow-covered tracks, through abandoned villages of derelict mud houses. We pass checkpoints and drive onwards. The radio station stands on the top of a mountain. There's a building at its highest point, where an American reconnaissance unit is quartered. The sides of the mountain are fenced off, guarded by Afghan soldiers under American supervision. They're probably listening in on our radio traffic as well. The radio station is situated in a draughty shed. We soon discover that one of the amplifier stages has frozen. Our European equipment isn't built for these kinds of temperatures. The technicians swap out a module, now our phone calls in camp will be clear and easy to understand again. On the way back we get into a snowstorm. I'm afraid that we'll get stuck somewhere on our route and have to spend the night in an ice-cold vehicle, but, though it's late in the evening, we make it back to camp.

Before I go to sleep, I read in Emerson: ... *because we are entitled to these enlargements, and, once having passed the bounds, shall never again be quite the miserable pedants we were.*

Wednesday 18 February 2004

For five weeks, no entries in my diary, no letter from Theresa. I have had the flu, and Sergei sat at my bedside during the bouts of fever. I tell him about my father, Sabine, Theresa. I don't have the courage to tell him about Jan.

When I'm well again, I telephone my mother. She is seriously planning to move with her new guy to Hamburg. I don't know how I'm supposed to feel about that, but honestly it doesn't bother me, she should do what she wants. If she lives in Hamburg, she'll be near to Sabine. Perhaps that would be good for my sister.

In the Eifel spring has already made its entrance, but here it is extremely cold, great quantities of snow still lie on the ground. If it all melts in a short space of time there are bound to be major floods. Does Theresa think of me sometimes? She will be disappointed I have not come home.

Theresa and Bruni had painted the large barn together over the last few days. The yard smelled of wood preserver; by the evening their eyes were streaming and their wrists ached. Now that the horses were back standing out in the fields, at least there was less to do in the stables. Kessler had announced that during the holidays children would again be coming to ride. After they had put the horses for the riding pupils on to the pasture, they inspected the fences every morning and checked they had the full complement of animals. The grass was wet with dew, Theresa's shoes were soaked through after a couple of metres, and she was annoyed with herself for not having worn her boots. As she climbed up the slope, the sun poked out from behind the mountain top and warmed her pleasantly. Ever since Bruni had found out how well Theresa and Justus hit it off, she had constantly found fault with Theresa and taken every opportunity to badmouth her in front of Kessler. Cars drove along the country road, mostly people on their way to work. There was a lava quarry on the hillside on the other side of the valley, and from time to time you heard the howling of the digger, which was loading lava stone on to a trailer. Justus turned his practice vehicle into the yard. One of the horses was lame, an abscess in its hoof, probably. They had been with the horse last night, and Kessler had said he wanted to call the vet because the hoof had suddenly become inflamed. Justus parked in front of the barn, got out and grabbed his medical bag from the back seat. Justus was short and stocky, he swung his arms around as he walked, he looked older than he was, but Theresa liked him and she would have loved to run down to him and hug him and kiss him. She thought she could see that he was scanning the yard for her, before he stepped into the stable with Bruni. Theresa walked on up towards the top of the hill where the horses were grazing. Fortunately, none had broken out, they were stood peacefully in the pasture and ran towards her as she approached. She climbed over the fence and followed the well-worn track, the horses trotting along behind her. The path led to the top of the hill, past a fenced-off crater and copses of trees. At the summit she had to climb over a rusty barbed-wire fence, then she could see the glittering maar in the valley below. She lay down on her stomach and rested her chin on her hands. The maar was deep and round; to her it looked like the murky eye of a sweet-tempered giant looking into the sky as it dreamed. Over the maar she saw swallows, which had just come back to the Eifel from God knows where to breed and raise their young. She thought of Paul and the peculiar things he had been writing to her recently. She needed to say to him, finally, that it was over for her, though perhaps he knew that already. At the weekend she would have free time, she wanted to drive to Jan's, he was going to have to have another operation. She remembered how she had camped down there on the shore of the lake with Paul and Jan, how they had swum out into the maar.

Monday 15 March 2004

The melting snow and constant rain in the last few days have caused floods across the region. At one bridge we get bogged down. Animal carcasses lie in the mud, human corpses, covered with carpets, are lined up on the sides of the road. Many people have caught leptospirosis through contact with the urine, blood or tissue of rats or mice. In one village the foul water stood so high in the huts that a child would have drowned in it. The inhabitants have to wade through the water to our ambulance. We supply them with medicine and provisions as best we can. It's impossible to help everyone here.

In a short break I see common terns (*Sterna hirundo*). They are on the homeward migration of their long journey around the globe. They are wearing their nuptial plumage, their beaks are coloured red, a black cap sits on their white heads, while the rest of their plumage, including their lance-like tails, is white. They hover in one spot over the water, dart down to dive for fish. I am amazed at how they can make out any fish at all in that brown broth.

After our mission it is time to clean our medical equipment and weapons and repair our uniforms. I sleep for a long time. No more dreams, thank God. I'm afraid of my dreams now.

I am on my lookout post and think I see a white sailing boat on my lake, which has grown huge with the melting snow and rainfall of the last few weeks. Birds on their migration home make a brief rest stop at the lake. I so want to go there to say my farewells to this country.

And now the foxes have reappeared in the prohibited area, they are shedding their winter coats, they look as dishevelled as wandering beggars. Given that they haven't set off the alarm, either the electronic barrier has been switched off or it's been put out of action by the volume of snow. Lucky for the foxes, who would otherwise have been shot by the guards. Julian watches me suspiciously, sometimes he follows me as I roam around the camp. Apparently he reckons that I want to go back to the lake. Julian trails after me when I walk to the tower, or I'll see him walking past, as if by chance, when I'm sitting by the Hesco wall and watching birds. I can't stand the way he looks at me, the way he's treating me, for much longer. He says he doesn't want to share a room with a deserter who could ruin his career, he threatens me, says he'll tie me to my bed at night if he has to.

Common tern (*Sterna hirundo*)

Wednesday 7 April 2004

Spring has come, and suddenly fresh greenery is sprouting everywhere. On a patrol we take a break in the vicinity of what was once a magnificent seat of government, its gardens are overgrown and circled by tank traps and wire mesh, the façade is pocked with bullet holes. I abandon the convoy, walk off completely alone, far away from my comrades, walking in a straight line, worm my way through a barbed-wire fence with my rifle at the ready, climb up the slope which leads to the palace. A long time ago there must have been fierce skirmishes here, which resulted ultimately in the palace being overrun. The victors tore out doors and windows, the furnishings were tossed into the garden. The foyer and all the other rooms are completely empty, the elaborate plasterwork has been smashed off the walls, in one room putrefied body parts lie, as if someone has dragged them there and piled them up.

I leave the palace and sit down on a chair in the garden. No one in my troop has noticed my absence. I hear something rustling and see a Russian tortoise in the grass, now in the springtime it's crawling back out of its burrow. Some of my comrades in the camp keep them as pets, they have arranged a grove of honour for our fallen comrades, in which twelve of these tortoises have a small enclosure and are fed on salad leaves.

What is Theresa doing right now? During our last phone call she told me that she was about to sit the exam to become a qualified groom, because of her work at the stud farm she hadn't got around to studying much, but Justus has been helping her with it. She mentions his name again and again. White-tailed and red-tailed bumblebees fly around buzzing in the sunshine, butterflies flutter and settle on the profusion of tulips of many colours. With my weapon at the ready I walk around the grounds, bumping into blossoming apricot trees, quince trees, pear trees, peach trees and plum trees. Large birdhouses stand on plinths of brick, smaller ones with elaborately wrought bars hang in the crowns of the trees. I don't see a single bird in this garden, but I can hear them.

Thursday 20 May 2004

It's turned very hot now, and the Dead Sea sparrows are breeding again on the old Russian armoured personnel carrier. Unlike when I first arrived here, the heat no longer bothers me. In a few days the young will hatch out.

In the past year I have seen over 137 species of bird, of which thirty-five have been first sightings. Over the winter, I did a lot of work on my book of feathers, I have stowed the feathers, drawings and notes away in one of the sturdy aluminium boxes.

I've been in the library container almost every day during the last few months. How frequently I dreamed of my lake, how often I was on its shore in my thoughts, I don't know any more. I have read a great deal, made numerous notes. Stuff I don't myself understand when I re-read it. Perhaps Ambrosius never left the Eifel, perhaps he just lived a few villages away from Kall with a secret mistress.

Of Ambrosius's old property only the barn on the bank of the river still stood. When I opened the door a crack and squeezed through, I found myself in a twilight, bygone world, where what had been before me had dissolved into dust and yet somehow had not ceased to exist. I could still guess at everything, I stumbled through the barn, stubbing the toes of my shoes against metal canisters on the earth floor. There were farm implements everywhere, knapsacks of brindled cow skin hung from the stone walls, an old bridle and a bucket full of rusty screws, nails and metal casings. A soil-encrusted harrow on a trailer stood under a raised wooden threshing floor, the river gurgled outside and sunlight fell through cracks in the roof in strips of glowing and dancing dust. I heard the shrill calls of the circling swallow from the river. Quietly, fearfully, I counted up what I knew and did not know, what I would never experience, what I might perhaps see and then forget again, what I might hide forever, leave buried in my memory. Somewhere in this barn there must be something of Ambrosius still, something that was more than just a story. I found it on the raised threshing floor – Ambrosius's flying suit hung over a beam like the slack winged pelt of a huge primeval bird. Perhaps with this I would finally be able to take flight. I climbed up the ladder to the threshing floor, stood on tiptoe and reached for the flying suit. Just as I grabbed hold of the edge of the suit, the frail planks gave way beneath me. I plunged downwards, my feet were jammed into a hole, I braced myself against the floor with my arms to stop myself from falling on to the harrow. I was trapped under the flying suit, which had floated down and spread itself over me. I could hardly breathe, I was in the clutches of a strange beast, which seemed to have lain in wait for me in that barn for centuries. In the dusty darkness, for the first time I was afraid of dying and of death. I imagined how the tines of the harrow beneath me would stab into my back, jut out through my eyes, my mouth, my neck. The crumbling floorboards creaked at the slightest movement.

It was evening by the time I finally freed my head from the suit, which turned out in reality to be a military overcoat of dusty felt. Exhausted I lay on the wooden floor, pale moonlight fell through the shed on to a kitbag, a sextant, yellowed maps and books, a wooden chest on a ledge. In the chest were yellowed sheets of parchment with a language of words that had crumbled to dust. I tore up the pages, opened the door of the shed and threw the scraps of parchment into the river glittering in the moonlight, kept only my memory.

Barn swallow (*Hirundo rustica*)

Friday 21 May 2004

It is getting more and more dangerous. Every day new horror stories reach us about attacks in the region – though mostly they affect native militias or civilians. I lie on my bed and think about how I will be flying home in a few days, my national service over. In the winter term I will start a biology degree. I have saved enough money from my pay to finance the degree, if I live a reasonably frugal life. I will see Theresa and Jan again. At some point, when this war is over, I would like to come back here, meet Nassim again and travel through this formidable country, look at the birds, as Ambrosius did, and describe them. I will compile a book on the birdlife of Afghanistan, there's hardly any literature on this country's birds. That's what I'm dreaming about when Sergei appears in the container, he's brought a letter from Theresa from the post office and he throws it at me.

Saturday 22 May 2004

She went for a stroll with Jan, Theresa writes. He could walk almost normally again. It was a beautiful day, the sun was shining gently. She had spent the whole of the previous night keeping watch at the stud farm, because one of mares was foaling. Early in the morning Bruni drove her on the scooter to Gerolstein, and on the train she fell asleep from exhaustion and only woke up shortly before Kall. She ran from the station to Jan's parents' house to pick him up. She had been looking forward to this free day with him. He had covered the bandage on his head, which he'd had to wear since the operation, with a woollen hat, Jan's eyes looked to her almost as mischievous and full of intelligent questions as they had before. Odette gave them a packed lunch and a vacuum flask of coffee. Theresa describes how they strolled through the Urfttal. For the first time, she says, Jan spoke a few sentences. He was still plodding a little, but as they walked he formed short sentences: that is a tree, that is a pebble, that is a puddle, there are clouds, the birds are singing. Sometimes Jan stood still and looked around him, like a small child who sees everything for the first time with curious eyes, he glanced up at the sky and pointed at something. But I didn't know what he meant, she writes. They reached the Roman well head. Perhaps she had asked too much of him, but he had shown no sign of exhaustion and even wanted to carry on walking further, until suddenly he collapsed next to her. He was lying in the grass next to the Medusa, his arms and legs and eventually his whole body were convulsed with spasms. Theresa didn't know what she should do, there was no one there who could help her. All the time he was stammering her name. She was alone with him. She called the ambulance and Odette. By the time they arrived, Jan was already dead.

Sunday 23 May 2004

I must have screamed and started crying after I read the letter. My comrades were standing right in front of my bed throwing darts. I can still feel the dart whizzing past me as I suddenly sat up. 'What's up with you, Paul?' snapped Sergei. I heard the shaft of the dart vibrating in the cork. Since that moment I've been hearing peculiar things. I lay awake the whole night. I can only think about Jan, about the fact that it was me driving the vehicle. I don't know what time means here, and it's not clear to me why I should go back home, now I've lost Theresa and Jan. In this state I wander through the camp. Julian pursues me, Sergei has to go off on a mission. I roam the whole of Sunday, walk up to the Soviet tanks. The tortoises in the grove of honour have long since disappeared into their burrows. I attend morning mass, I don't know what makes me do that because I've not even once been to Sunday prayers in the camp, perhaps I think that at least Julian won't follow me there. Back in the container I read Theresa's letter again. I scream at Julian when he steps into our dorm, I yell at him, finally he should leave me in peace. We start to fight, I'm taking swings at him, he doesn't fight back, assures me he only wants to help me, laughs at my feeble attempts to hurt him. But then I do hit him, so that he stumbles, falls to the floor, bangs his head against the bed frame and lies there unconscious. Against express orders, I leave the camp. I climb over the Hesco wall, cross the prohibited area on hands and knees, crawl under the fence, run across fields, which since I was last there have been peppered with craters of swampy, stinking water. I run onwards to the shore of the lake, pull off my flak jacket, strip off my shirt. Now I stand on the shore and spread my arms.

After Helena had sorted and filed the pages by date, a few sheets were left over – mostly lists of bird observations, notes she could not understand, which Paul had evidently written in his confused state after he had absconded from the camp. The ink on some of the drawings and diary entries had run in the wet, and she could not decipher them. She thought she could make out in these pages that Paul had found Nassim in the lake and had only been able to identify him by his father's binoculars. Paul had pulled Nassim out of the lake and buried him behind the ruined wall where they had sat together. Then Paul had headed off further and further away from the camp. Only meagre scraps of text survived from this time. Paul, it seemed, had wandered aimlessly across Afghanistan, over mountain passes and across lonely steppe. Afghan farmers had given him food. Helena had to put it all together like a jigsaw.

An American helicopter spotted him months later, on a steppe near the border with Pakistan. He was crouched on a mound of earth near to a small lake. The Americans took him into custody, flew him to their camp. They assumed that this strange, bearded man in uniform was a soldier who had gone over to al-Qaeda. In his rucksack they found diaries and drawings. Soon the Americans realised they had only a harmless lunatic on their hands. Eventually they handed Paul over to the German army.

Paul spent the weeks before the flight home in the sick bay at the camp, he sat on his camp bed, made notes and sometimes mimicked the voices of birds. Sergei and Julian visited him, brought him feathers that his comrades had found on operations. The fate of Paul Arimond was a theme in the bar every evening. A few days before the flight back home, his mental state improved. It was possible to speak normally with him again. One morning the next contingent of soldiers returning home stepped on to the bus that would carry them from the camp to the airport on the edge of the city. Paul sat in silence next to Sergei by the window, and he did not once look out as the road ran for a short stretch past the lake.

9.6.2004 Attack on German Army soldiers (dpa) Four German soldiers have died in a bus near to the Afghan capital Kabul. According to the Ministry of Defence in Berlin, ten men were also severely injured in the explosion and twenty were slightly injured, including civilians. The International Security Assistance Force (ISAF) said it was a 'targeted attack'. The bus carrying German members of ISAF was near the German base on the Jalalabad road heading towards the city centre when the explosion occurred. The deputy commander of Afghan troops in Kabul considered it was most likely a suicide attack using a car. Eyewitnesses saw the two suspected attackers in a taxi, which was following the bus before the detonation. The German soldiers had completed their missions in Afghanistan and were on the way to Kabul airport, from where they were due to catch their flights home.

My father had marked his start line on the carriageway and spray-painted a dot where he had to increase his speed and run on the diagonal up to the railing. He tested the wind direction. There was hardly any traffic so early in the morning and, besides, back then the motorway ended a few kilometres beyond the bridge and after that you had to carry on southwards through the Eifel on bumpy country roads. Mist rose up from the valley; falcons soared in the clear air above. Below, on the valley floor, in trees and bushes, birds were singing now, my father heard their faint melodies as he pressed his eyes closed to walk through his jump in his mind once more. He had a light headwind, but that was helpful for his take-off and flight. He retied his shoelaces, pranced on his tiptoes, tested the wind direction a final time and looked around him. As he set off, a car came into view, approaching at high speed. Now he was running on the diagonal at maximum acceleration up to his take-off point, just before the railing he shortened his stride, set the front of his left foot down, pushed away, pivoted at the same time on his own axis, his arms were stretched upwards, they pointed in the direction of the imaginary magic line, he turned on to his back, looked into the sky and took off.

Acknowledgements

In the winter months of 2005–6 a conspicuous guest visited the small café in the supermarket in Kall, a bearded young man who wore threadbare corduroy trousers and a German army parka several sizes too large with its insignia cut off. He sat most of the time in a corner by the window and had a small tortoise sitting next to him on the bench, a tortoise he had previously lifted out of the box on his bicycle, tucked into his woollen satchel and carried into the café. When I engaged this young man in conversation for the first time, naturally I asked him about his tortoise. It was, he explained, a Russian tortoise (*Testudo horsfieldii Gray*, 1844). The young man knew a great deal about biology; every animal he mentioned in our conversations he called by its correct Latin name.

In the spring of 2006 the Tortoise-Man stopped coming to the café. It seemed he had disappeared from our part of the world, because after that I never encountered him again; what remained is his story. Perhaps our story is the only part of us that does remain. I am grateful to the Tortoise-Man for his tales. But tales are one thing, reality is another, it shapes the story and affects it from within. In the case of this novel, set in Afghanistan, the research process was arduous and not without its problems. Which is why my contact with Frank Joisten and Thomas Rubner was such a stroke of luck. Frank Joisten completed three deployments with the German army in Kabul, Mazar-i-Sharif, Pul-i-Khumri, Kunduz, Fayzabad and the Wakhan Corridor. Like my protagonist Paul Arimond, he made ornithological observations during his missions and collaborated on them with German universities. For my introduction to Frank Joisten I have to thank Professor

Gunther Nogge. A long time ago, Professor Nogge was director of Kabul Zoo. Just at the moment when the idea for my book was ripening and I was beginning to research the zoology of Afghanistan, he and Dr Ehsan Arghandewal published their book *Afghanistan zoologisch betrachtet* (*The Zoology of Afghanistan*). This wonderful book at last made it possible for me to write my novel. Professor Nogge also drew my attention to the labours of Frank Joisten.

Alongside these particular sources, I want to thank the authors of many non-fiction works on Afghanistan, be they in book form or in blogs. I was only able to make my novel a reality on the strength of all of these sources. The books, articles and webpages I read for this project are cited individually in the bibliography. I would like to thank in addition Dr Andreas Erb, Melanie David, Arno E. Chun, Dietrich Schubert, Dr Nina Benkert, Monika Alt, Gregor Seferens, Corinna Kroker, Herbert Homberger, Bettina Seng and Dr Raimund Bezold. For the structure and pattern of the novel, I owe particular thanks to my editor Professor Martin Hielscher, for all that pertains to life and literature, to my beloved wife Elvira, for the beautiful coffee watercolours and for discussions, to my son Erasmus. Without all these friends and acquaintances, it would not have been possible for me to write *The Language of Birds*, or at any rate not in the form in which it now presents itself to you.

Norbert Scheuer
Kall, 22 November 2014

Glossary

BAT stands for Beweglicher Arzttrupp (mobile medical troop), a military unit in the German army offering emergency medical first aid.

BASTARD WING / ALULA is a tuft of feathers on the leading edge of a bird's wing. These feathers are tilted upwards during flight manoeuvres such as braking or cornering to stabilise the airflow. Birds that perform these kinds of aerial manoeuvre especially often – forest-dwellers, for example – have a correspondingly large tuft of feathers.

DINGO is an armoured and armed reconnaissance vehicle.

ISAF stands for the International Security Assistance Force. ISAF was led by NATO and existed between 2001 and 2014.

HESCO WALL / HESCO BASTION WALL is a wall made of cuboid wire cages, 1.2 metres across, filled with ballast and used for military fortifications to defend against enemy bombardment.

FUCHS (FOX) ARMOURED PERSONNEL CARRIER is an amphibious armoured vehicle. It is used mainly to transport personnel and equipment.

Note

The birds described in the book are either native to Afghanistan or are seen there on migration. Professor Nogge and Frank Joisten have pointed out to me that the Dead Sea sparrow has not yet been seen in the north of Afghanistan.

Given that the camp described in the text is a literary location, which might be transferred from Afghanistan to other war zones, I have in this one case, for purely literary reasons, disregarded scientific fact.

Bibliography

English-language editions are listed where available.

AG Friedensforschung: Afghanistan: Kriegschronik. In
collaboration with Katharina Leinius. Accessible online at www.
ag-friedensforschung.de/regionen/Afghanistan/Welcome.html,
last accessed 30.07.2018

Baumann, Marc, Mauritius Much, Bastian Obermayer, Martin
Langeder, Franziska Storz, *Feldpost. Briefe deutscher Soldaten aus
Afghanistan*. Reinbek 2011

Bellow, Saul, *Dangling Man*. London 2006 (first published 1944)

Bezzel, Einhard, *Vogelfedern: Federn heimischer Arten nach Farben
bestimmen*. Munich 2010

Bouvier, Nicolas, *The Way of the World*. London 2007 (first published
in French 1963)

Clair, Johannes, *Vier Tage im November: Mein Kampfeinsatz in
Afghanistan*. Berlin 2012

Conradi, Arnulf, *Kleine Philosophie der Passionen: Vögel*. Munich
1998

Derrida, Jacques, *Writing and Difference*. London 1978 (first
published in French 1967)

Dierschke, Volker, *Welcher Vogel ist das? 170 Vögel einfach bestimmen*.
Stuttgart 2009

Emerson, Ralph Waldo, *Nature and Selected Essays*. London 2003
(first published 1836)

Erös, Reinhard, *Unter Taliban, Warlords und Drogenbaronen: Eine
deutsche Familie kämpft für Afghanistan*. Hamburg 2008

Foucault, Michel, *Discipline and Punish: The Birth of the Prison*. London 1977 (first published in French 1975)

Goethe, Johann Wolfgang, *Dichtung und Wahrheit*. Jörn Göres (ed). Frankfurt am Main 2000 (first published 1811–1833)

Groos, Heike, *Ein schöner Tag zum Sterben: Als Bundeswehrärztin in Afghanistan*. Frankfurt am Main 2009

Groos, Heike, *"Das ist auch euer Krieg!": Deutsche Soldaten berichten von ihren Einsätzen*. Frankfurt am Main 2011

Haag, Holger, *Welcher Vogel ist das? Strand und Küste: 78 Arten einfach bestimmen*. Stuttgart 2013

Kant, Immanuel, *Critique of Pure Reason*. Cambridge 1999 (first published 1781)

Kant, Immanuel, *Werkausgabe*. 12 vols. Frankfurt am Main 2004 (first published 1768)

Lohmann, Michael, *Singvögel: Vorkommen, Lebensweise, Gesang*. Munich 2012

Malouf, David, *Fly Away Peter*. London 1999

Martinet, François Nicolas, *Geschichte der Vögel: In allen sicht und wahrnehmbaren Merkmalen abgebildet*. Potsdam 2011

NABU – Naturschutzbund Deutschland e.V: Accessible online at www.nabu.de

Naumann, Johann Friedrich, *Die Vögel Mitteleuropas: Eine Auswahl*. Frankfurt am Main 2009

Nogge, Gunther, *Afghanistan zoologisch betrachtet*. Bonn 2012

Plato, *Sämtliche Dialoge*, Otto Apelt, Kurt Hildebrandt, Constantin Ritter, Gustav Schneider (eds). Hamburg 1988

Pliny the Elder, *Natural History*, John F. Healy (ed). London 1991 (first published 77–79 CE)

Polo, Marco, *The Travels*. London 2016

Polo, Marco, *Il Milione: Die Wunder der Welt: Übersetzung aus altfranzösichen Quellen und Nachwort*. Zürich 1983

Reichholf, Josef H., *Der Ursprung der Schönheit: Darwins größtes Dilemma*. Munich 2011

———

Riechelmann, Cord, Judith Schalansky (eds), *Krähen: Ein Portrait*. Berlin 2013

Roché, Jean C., *Bird Songs and Calls of Britain and Europe*. Audiobook on 4 CDs. London 1996

Rothenberg, David, *Why Birds Sing: A Journey into the Mystery of Bird Song*. London 2006

Scheffner, Philip (director), *The Halfmoon Files*. Film. Berlin 2013

Schetter, Conrad J., *Kleine Geschichte Afghanistans*. Munich 2010

Schwittek, Peter, *In Afghanistan*. Zürich 2011

Serres, Michel, *The Five Senses: A Philosophy of Mingled Bodies*. London 2008

Svensson, Lars, Killian Mullarney, Dan Zetterström, *Collins Bird Guide: The Most Complete Guide to the Birds of Britain and Europe*. London 2010 (updated 2015)

Tait, Malcolm, Olive Tayler, *The Birdwatcher's Companion: Winged Wonders, Fantastic Flocks and Outstanding Ornithology*. London 2005

Thoreau, Henry David, *Civil Disobedience and Reading*. London 1995 (first published 1849)

Thoreau, Henry David, *Walden*. London 2016 (first published 1854)

Tomiak, Kerstin, *Drachenwind: Mein Jahr in Afghanistan*. Munich 2009

Trouern-Trend, Jonathan, *Birding Babylon: A Soldier's Journal from Iraq*. San Francisco 2006

Walser, Robert, *Jakob von Gunten*. New York 1999

Willemsen, Roger, *An Afghan Journey*. London 2007

Wohlgethan, Achim, *Operation Kundus: Mein zweiter Einsatz in Afghanistan*. Berlin 2011